A Fairytale Christmas

Meet the McKenzie sisters—
twins who couldn't be more different if they tried!

Dreamy single mom Gwen secretly longs for
a happy-ever-after for herself and her adorable
baby, Claire, but can she ever learn to trust again?

High-powered Gill craves professional success,
and has given up waiting for Prince Charming
to sweep her off her stilettos. Except this year,
does fate have a surprise in store…?

With some Christmas magic, these sisters
are about to meet the men of their dreams!

Find out how in two fabulous linked stories
by popular author
Susan Meier
and introducing brand-new author
Barbara Wallace!

SUSAN MEIER
BARBARA WALLACE

A Fairytale Christmas

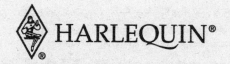

TORONTO • NEW YORK • LONDON
AMSTERDAM • PARIS • SYDNEY • HAMBURG
STOCKHOLM • ATHENS • TOKYO • MILAN • MADRID
PRAGUE • WARSAW • BUDAPEST • AUCKLAND

ISBN-13: 978-0-373-17693-9

A FAIRYTALE CHRISTMAS

First North American Publication 2010

Copyright © 2010 by Harlequin Books S.A.

The publisher acknowledges the copyright holders of the individual works as follows:

BABY BENEATH THE CHRISTMAS TREE
Copyright © 2010 by Linda Susan Meier

MAGIC UNDER THE MISTLETOE
Copyright © 2010 by Barbara Wallace

Recycling programs for this product may not exist in your area.

For questions and comments about the quality of this book please contact us at Customer_eCare@Harlequin.ca.

www.eHarlequin.com

Printed in U.S.A.

SUSAN MEIER

Baby Beneath the Christmas Tree

Dear Reader,

When I was offered the opportunity to write this anthology, and was asked if there was a newer writer I'd like to work with, I didn't even hesitate. I instantly said Barbara Wallace!

I met Barbara at the Romance Writers of America national conference. Not only was she pretty, but she was also sweet and kind. I knew those qualities would translate into a great story. And they did. Barbara created a wonderful twin sister for my heroine, and put Gill in a romance readers will long remember.

It's always fun to write about Christmas. I believe it's a magical time of the year. I got a chance to really expand on that theme by setting "Baby Beneath the Christmas Tree" on a Christmas tree farm. Gwen and Drew are made for each other, but neither sees that because there are too many complications in their lives. Gwen is a young single mom, desperate to finish her degree and be able to support her child. CEO Drew is an absentee dad, getting a second chance with the sixteen-year-old son he barely knows.

They have an age difference, a class difference and even a totally different outlook on life. So it's more than magic when they realize each can solve the other's problem. But solving problems is one thing. Getting the courage to take another chance on love when each has been hurt before is quite another. And maybe, just maybe, they'll get some extra-special help from the spirit that permeates Teaberry Farms.

I hope you enjoy "Baby Beneath the Christmas Tree" as much as I enjoyed writing it! To an author every book is special, but for me this one truly is magic.

Susan Meier

* * *

To my friend Denise, who listens to
every incarnation of every story long before I write it!

CHAPTER ONE

FOR as long as Gwendolyn McKenzie could remember the old timers in the tiny town of Towering Pines, West Virginia, had whispered that Teaberry Farms was enchanted. The rumor was that if you touched one of the Teaberry Christmas trees while wishing, your wish would come true.

Driving up the fir-lined mountain road that took her to the farm, Gwen glanced around in amazement, understanding why the legend had formed. Majestic evergreens punched into a vast indigo sky. Fat, fluffy white snowflakes pirouetted around the green pine branches, falling heavily, like frosting on sugar cookies, creating a magical world.

But when she reached the Teaberry mansion, Gwen's mouth dropped open in dismay. Two rows of tall windows with thin black shutters dominated the huge redbrick home, but the shutters tilted drunkenly from age and neglect. The Teaberry family hadn't even visited for at least a decade, so it didn't surprise her that the house was in disrepair. But she'd thought Andrew Teaberry, her new boss, would have called ahead to have the place prepared to be used. If the house was this bad on the outside, she feared it would be worse on the inside.

Still, a wisp of smoke rose from the redbrick chimney, disappearing into the inky sky, proof that the caretaker must have started a fire in preparation for the owner's return. At least she and her daughter wouldn't spend their time shivering while they waited for Andrew to arrive.

She got out of her beat-up little red car, opened the back door and reached in to unbuckle the car seat of her three-month-old baby. When she'd gotten pregnant by a boyfriend who'd bolted the very second she'd told him, Gwen and her twin sister Gill had both worried that she might fall into the same trap their mom had. Ginger McKenzie had married the man who had gotten *her* pregnant. But when twins were born he'd panicked, saying one baby was difficult enough to handle, two was impossible. He left town, leaving Ginger to raise the girls alone, watching out the window, longing for him to come home.

Six months after her mom's sudden death, finding herself in a position very close to Ginger's, Gwen had quickly shaped up. She didn't want to be one of those women who wasted her entire life pining after a man who didn't want her. She'd stopped believing in miracles. She'd stopped believing wishes came true. She'd packed away her dreamy side. And she now only dealt in facts.

Which was why she was at this rundown old house, about to start a job as the assistant to a man she'd never met. She had to pay her own way, support a child and finish her degree. This job might be temporary, but it paid enough money that if she watched how she spent she could keep herself and Claire through her last semester of university.

"Hey, Claire-bear," she said, lifting the little girl and rubbing noses. Bundled in her thick pink snowsuit, with the white fur of the hood framing her face, chubby, happy Claire really did look something like a stuffed pink bear.

Using the key sent to her by Andrew Teaberry, Gwen unlocked the front door and stepped inside. A huge curving mahogany staircase greeted her and Claire. But so did cobwebs. A layer of dust coated the banister and the stairs.

"Wow. We could be in big trouble, Claire-bear."

Walking from room to room, she felt her dismay grow. Though the lights worked, the sinks had water and the kitchen appliances had been plugged into electrical outlets and hummed with life, the house was filthy. Her boss might have instructed the caretaker to get the utilities turned on and the furnace working, but he'd forgotten about cleaning.

Discovering a suite in the back that had probably at one time been the maid's quarters, Gwen set Claire's baby carrier on the dusty bare mattress of the single bed, but then lifted it up again. She'd arrived an hour early, hoping to make a good impression, but Andrew hadn't yet arrived. If she hurried, she could race home for a vacuum cleaner, mop, broom, soap and dustcloths, and still have time to clean this suite enough that Claire could sleep here.

Two hours later, Andrew Teaberry pulled his shiny black SUV into the circular driveway in front of his family's old homestead and his face fell in disgust. Pressed for time on this spur-of-the-moment trip, he'd thought ahead enough to hire an assistant and have the caretaker open the place, but he hadn't considered that the Teaberry mansion might not be habitable.

"So this is the fabulous Teaberry Farms." In the passenger's seat of the SUV, Drew's sixteen-year-old son Brody glanced around and snorted with derision. "Looks like a rat-hole to me."

Drew nearly squeezed his eyes shut in frustration. As if it wasn't bad enough that he had to move into this old monstrosity while he negotiated the purchase of a local manufacturing company, his ex-wife had decided to get remarried, forcing

Drew to keep their son for the entire month of her honeymoon. So while he negotiated to buy the business of crusty old Jimmy Lane, a West Virginia entrepreneur who only wanted to sell his business to someone who lived in West Virginia, he was saddled with a sassy sixteen-year-old.

Inserting the key into the back door lock, he glanced behind him at Brody, who was so engrossed in whatever he was doing with his cell phone that he didn't even watch where he walked. Wearing a black knit cap over his yellow hair, and a thick parka that seemed to swallow him whole, Brody was the complete opposite of his dark-haired, dark-eyed, always observant dad. The kid was going to step into traffic one day.

Brushing up against one of the pine trees beside the kitchen door as he pulled the key out of the door lock, Drew prayed that they both survived this month. He pushed open the door, stepped into a kitchen that looked like something out of a horror movie and froze.

"Mr. Teaberry!" The woman standing by the dusty kitchen counter winced. "I'd say welcome home, but I'm not sure that's exactly appropriate, given the condition of the place."

Drew blinked at yet another surprise this morning. Unless she was Max Peabody, the caretaker, this had to be his temporary administrative assistant, Gwen McKenzie. In their phone interview she'd told him she had one more semester of university to finish, so he'd pictured her as being a petite sprite, someone who'd look only a little older than his son. Instead he'd hired a classically beautiful woman with thick blond hair and catlike green eyes, who was built like every man's fantasy come to life. A bright red sweater accented her ample bosom. Dark, low-riding jeans caressed her perfect bottom. Her shoulder-length hair swung when she moved.

He slid his laptop onto an available counter, glancing around at the nightmare of a kitchen. The oak cabinets were solid, but coated in dust, as were the kitchen table and the four chairs around it. But, like the cabinets, the furniture and the ceramic floor tiles looked to be in good shape. The house wasn't really falling apart, just dirty.

"Good morning. Sorry we're late. We couldn't get on the road until hours after we'd planned."

She batted her hand in dismissal. "Not a problem."

Brody pushed into the kitchen behind his dad, not caring that he'd bumped into him. "Hey, babe, thought for sure you'd have muffins and coffee waiting."

Drew blanched at his son's disrespect. "Not only is Gwen not our cook, but we don't call employees *babe*."

"All right. Great. No babe." Brody pulled his sunglasses down his nose and peered over the rim at Gwen. "Sorry about that, sweetie."

"We don't call employees sweetie, either!" Drew said, his temperature rising. If he didn't know better, he'd think the kid was deliberately antagonizing him. "How about an apology?"

Brody glared at his dad. "Fine. I'm sorry. Why don't you just write a list of rules so I know what I can and can't say this next month?"

With that he stormed through the kitchen, all but knocking the swinging door off its hinges as he punched through it.

Though Drew knew he should go after him, he had no idea what to say to this new version of Brody. That was part of the problem. Sixteen years ago, when his ex had moved herself and their son to Colorado, two thousand miles away from Drew, he'd protested. But in the end she hadn't budged, and his visits with Brody had become something like two-week vacations, spent on tropical islands or at ski resorts.

They'd always gotten along well. Until this trip. Now, Brody was suddenly obnoxious. Drew had absolutely no idea what the heck he was going to do with him for the entire month of December. One-on-one in a house so far out in the country that it didn't get cable TV, they were going to be miserable. Especially since Drew wasn't even sure when or why Brody had turned into such a mouthy kid or where to start with discipline.

He did, however, know exactly what to say to an embarrassed employee. He turned to Gwen. "I apologize for my son's behavior."

"Not a big deal," she said with a laugh. "He's what? Fifteen? Sixteen? He's testing the water. All kids do it."

A steamroller of relief rumbled through Drew. At least the relationship with his temporary administrative assistant would be normal. Then she smiled at him, her pretty green eyes shining, her full lips winging upward, and everything male inside of Drew responded. Her thick, shiny blond hair framed a heart-shaped face with bright eyes, a pert nose, and generous lips made for kissing.

Involuntarily, his gaze once again swept down the red sweater and tight jeans. He rarely went out, and when he did the women he dated were nothing like Gwen. They were tall, cool sophisticates. Models. Starlets. But there was no denying that this gorgeous blonde made him wonder what it would be like to kiss her—

He groaned inwardly. He wanted a normal working relationship with this woman! Plus, even if he was the kind to dabble in affairs, she was too young for him, and an employee. If those weren't enough, he had responsibilities as Chairman of the Board of his grandfather's conglomerate. The pressure of holding top position in a global company left him no time for anything but work. That was why he'd only spent vacations with Brody. Why Brody had had time to change without Drew even realizing. Why he had to figure out how he'd handle him for the four long weeks of December.

"I think I'll grab Brody and get our bags."

She winked. "Good idea."

Her wink was cute. Not flirty, but happy. And for some reason or another that sent a sizzle through Drew when he'd already reminded himself he wasn't allowed to be interested. Eager to get away from this confusing situation, he headed for the door that Brody had stormed through, and found himself in a hall and then a foyer, where Brody was bounding up the dusty steps.

He glanced around in renewed disgust. Cobwebs hung from the ceiling and created feathery loops on the walls. The house wasn't even clean enough to sleep in, but they had to stay here. There wasn't a hotel in tiny Towering Pines, and they were too far away from a city to drive back and forth. Plus, Jimmy Lane loved the idea that Drew was one of the original Teaberrys. He wanted to visit the Christmas tree farm. He wanted to see the mansion. Somehow or another Drew was going to have to make this place sparkle before his visit.

But as Brody stormed away Drew knew he'd have to deal with that later. "Hey! Aren't you going to help me with the bags?"

"Don't you have people for that?"

"Not here!" Drew yelled, as Brody continued up the steps. "Except for Ms. McKenzie, who's *my* assistant and not yours, we're on our own."

"Oh, I get it. *You* can use *Ms. McKenzie* for personal things, but I can't."

Something in the way Brody said that stopped Drew cold. Not because he shouldn't have an assistant, but because he was attracted to her. The entire time he'd been in the kitchen he'd kept losing his train of thought and stealing inappropriate looks at her.

Brody huffed out a sigh and started down the stairs. When he reached the bottom, Drew led him out the front door.

Stepping into the falling snow again, Drew headed toward his black SUV. The six inches that had blanketed West Virginia that morning gave the farm the look of a Currier and Ives painting. Even in disrepair, the big redbrick house had a solid, steady feel to it. Huge pines wrapped it in a warm embrace. Snow covered the fence and outbuildings, making everything sparkle.

Brody glanced around. "What a dump."

A sting of guilt whipped through Drew as he popped the hatch of the car. "Just because it isn't our cup of tea, that doesn't mean the farm is a dump."

"Whatever." Brody reached in and dragged his duffle bag out of the rear compartment. It fell into the snow with a thud. Brody sighed heavily. "What good is it to be rich if you have to carry your own luggage?"

Anger surged through Drew. "Life isn't only about comfort."

Yanking his duffle from the snow, Brody looked up over the rim of his sunglasses at his dad. "Whatever."

Drew knew he was in over his head with this kid, and he needed to fix this situation, fast.

CHAPTER TWO

GWEN heard Claire's soft cries through the small monitor she had on the kitchen counter. Without a second thought she turned and ran back into the hall, through the sitting room of the maid's quarters that she'd managed to clean before the Teaberrys arrived, and into the bedroom.

"Hey, Claire-bear. I'm here," she whispered, lifting her baby out of the portable crib. She kissed her warm cheek, changed her into a fresh one-piece sleeper and returned to the kitchen, fighting a funny feeling of confusion in the pit of her stomach.

For some reason or another she'd expected Andrew Teaberry to be older. Like sixty. Not thirty-five or so. She also hadn't expected fathomless dark eyes or gorgeous black hair. The hitch in her breath and the way her stomach had plummeted when she'd looked at him were also surprises.

Grabbing a bottle from the refrigerator, she told herself to stop thinking about how attractive her new employer was and get her baby fed and into her carrier before he returned from getting his bags. She wasn't sure how or where they'd work in this dusty house, but she wasn't assuming anything. From the way he'd instantly dealt with his son for calling her babe, it was clear he wasn't a man who took well to mistakes or assumptions. So she wouldn't make any.

She placed the bottle in the warmer she'd brought. As it heated, Claire began to cry. Gwen tried to comfort her, but her crying only grew louder.

"Come on, sweetie. I know you're hungry, but it will only take a minute to warm your bottle."

Just then the swinging door swung open and Drew burst inside. His horrified gaze fell to Claire, then swung back to Gwen. "Is that a baby?"

She laughed nervously. "Well, it's not a Siamese cat." She rocked her sobbing child, trying to get her to settle down. This was no way for him to meet her baby! "This is my daughter Claire."

He gaped at her. "You brought your baby to work?"

This time the flip-flop of Gwen's stomach had nothing to do with the attractiveness of her boss and everything to do with fear. "I told you about Claire in my interview."

"You told me you had a child. You didn't say you were bringing her with you."

Drew's loud voice caused Claire's crying to rise in competition. Gwen desperately rocked her, but the baby filled the room with her wails.

Gwen had to shout to be heard. "I did say she was still a bit too young to go to daycare and I don't have a sitter yet. I thought the conclusion was obvious."

"I thought you said that to let me know you needed time to look for a sitter." He raked his fingers through his hair. "I'm sorry, but I hired you because I need help. Serious help. You're not going to have time to care for a baby *and* do your work."

Gwen's heart stopped. *He was firing her?* He couldn't! She needed this job. "She's only three months old! She sleeps a lot. I can handle it."

He looked at the screaming baby, then bestowed a look upon Gwen that sent a shiver through her. "Really?"

Mustering her courage, she said, "Yes!"

"That's not how it looks to me. I know how this baby thing goes. I had a crying baby. Brody screamed for three months straight. I failed that semester of university. My wife left me—"

Just then the swinging door bounced closed. Gwen hadn't even realized it had been opened again. With Claire's crying and their heated conversation she'd missed Brody walking through the room.

Drew's face paled, then he squeezed his eyes shut. "Perfect." Heading for the door, he yelled, "Brody!" Then he pushed out of the kitchen.

The light on the bottle warmer finally declared the milk was warm, and Gwen took her baby to a chair to feed her.

This was not going anything like she'd hoped it would. She fed Claire and then sat at the table, totally confused about what she should do. Technically, Drew hadn't fired her. And she needed this job. She was not leaving without a fight.

Drew ran into the hallway just in time to see the foyer door close. He grabbed his jacket from the newel post on the stairs where he'd stashed it and headed outside.

Brody bounded toward the SUV around the side of the house.

"What are you going to do?" Drew shouted after his son. "Leave?" He dangled the keys. "You'll need these. Unless you want to walk."

"What do you care? Mom's on her honeymoon. You're trying to buy some old guy's company. And I'm stuck here."

"Look, Brody, if I had a choice we'd be skiing right now."

Brody snorted.

"We would." The heavy snow had reduced itself to flurries but it was cold. Bitter cold. And he had work to do. Not knowing what else to say, Drew glanced longingly at the kitchen door. Because the top half of the door was glass, he could see Gwen McKenzie at the table with her baby. He nearly groaned. Could this day get any more complicated?

"I'm sorry you heard what you heard, but truthfully I would have thought by now that you would have guessed your mom and I had a terrible marriage. We were only married for just under a year before we divorced."

Refusing to look at him, Brody said, "And I'm the cause."

"No!" He laughed miserably. "Lord, no. Your mom and I had lots of problems before you were born."

"But I added to them—"

"No!" Drew said again, this time stronger.

"I heard what you said about me screaming all the time."

"You were colicky. That happens. Babies do not destroy marriages. Adults do. Your mom and I never should have gotten married. But she got pregnant—"

Deliberately, she'd told him later. She'd taken out loans to attend her first semester at Harvard and had known four years' worth of borrowing that kind of money would put her too far in debt when she graduated. Drew's family was wealthy. He and Olivia had dated and liked each other. So she'd thought they'd be very happy raising a baby and attending university— all paid for by his parents. But his parents had been furious when Drew told them they had gotten married because she was pregnant, and they'd cut him off. The happy marriage that Olivia had envisioned had quickly become a nightmare.

Still, this wasn't the time or the way to tell Brody all that. And he wasn't even sure he should be the one to tell Brody.

It seemed this story would be much better coming from his mother.

"How about if we talk later? Right now, I have a mini-crisis in the kitchen."

Brody sighed and raised his face to the snow. It looked to Drew as if the cool flakes were settling him down, so when he said, "Go," Drew headed back to the kitchen.

With a deep calming breath of his own, he opened the kitchen door and stepped inside. "I'm sorry you had to see that."

Gwen McKenzie slowly raised her gaze to his, her green eyes wary.

He knew she needed this job. He didn't have to glance at the now sleeping baby to remember that, but he did, and his heart stuttered in his chest. He'd told Brody he had been colicky, but that had been only half the problem. Neither Drew nor Olivia had had any experience caring for an infant, and they'd had nowhere to turn for help. He knew how loudly a baby could cry, how despondent a parent could feel...how one tiny life really could throw a monkey wrench into the best-laid plans. And his plans to buy Jimmy Lane's company were precarious at best. Despite the efforts of most of his staff, he knew nothing about the owner of Lane Works except that he was reclusive and demanding. That didn't give Drew much to go on by way of figuring out how to handle him. So his "plan" was more like a guess.

"I'm sorry, but you having a baby here doesn't work for me."

Instead of the tears he'd expected, Gwen McKenzie shook her head and said, "No kidding."

He gaped at her. Had she just sassed him? Yes, she had. He'd already had a lifetime share of sassing this morning. So his voice shivered with barely controlled anger when he said, "Get your things and leave."

She rose from the chair. "Fine, but I would think that a guy who can't get along with his son would like having another parent around for some help and advice."

An unexpected laugh escaped him. "You think *you're* going to straighten out Brody?"

"Nope." She headed for the door. "But I might have some ideas for how you could."

He snorted in derision. "Right. You've been a parent now… what? All of two months?"

She turned and smiled. "Three. But I was sixteen only a few years ago. I think I might remember a bit more about what it was like than you do."

Drew's eyes narrowed and Gwen's stomach shivered. She knew she should probably shut up, but he was in trouble with Brody and that seemed like her only angle to keep this job. Now that he'd shrugged out of the thick parka, she could not only see his expensive blue sweater, she could also see that the body he'd hidden beneath his jacket was incredible. Soft knit hugged his broad shoulders and flat tummy and stopped at trim hips encased in denim. He was handsome, rich, and he held her fate in his hands…

And she was taunting him? Was she crazy?

"Are you calling me old?"

She should be. She should think that a guy in his midthirties was way too old for her. She should think he was too grouchy for her. Instead, all she saw was a handsome, sexy guy who needed her help. And, strangely, even with as many problems as she had of her own, she actually thought she could provide it.

She lifted her chin. Caught his gaze. "No. I'm not calling you old."

Their gazes clung. Time seemed to be suspended. She had a feeling she didn't have to tell him she didn't think he was old because she found him attractive. It was probably written all over her reddening face.

"But you do need me."

He crossed his arms on his chest as his gaze rippled over her. Suddenly feeling like a downtrodden waif, brought to the castle for the king's pleasure, Gwen cuddled Claire to her chest.

"You're dusty."

That wasn't at all what she'd expected him to say. So nervous her voice shook, she said, "I cleaned the maid's quarters so Claire would have somewhere to sleep."

He said nothing, only narrowed his eyes at her, as if trying to figure out if she was lying. So she hastily added, "I brought my vacuum, cleaning solutions and a bucket and mop from home."

"You know how to clean?"

She frowned. "Of course I know how to clean." A thought struck her and she said, "You don't?"

He shook his head.

Her spirits lifted. "There's another thing I could help you with."

He raked his fingers through his hair and looked at sleeping Claire again. She could almost see the wheels turning in his head as he drew the obvious conclusions. Claire wasn't a bad baby. Gwen knew how to clean. And this place was filthy.

"I won't even ask for more money."

His mouth dropped open, then he snorted a laugh. "Right. As if you're in a position to bargain."

"Come on," Gwen said, a slight note of feminine pleading in her voice. She instantly regretted it when his gaze caught hers and that "thing" sprang up between them again. The air she breathed turned hot and shivery. Something like electricity arched between them.

It was another item in the laundry list of problems they had. His son was trouble. The house wasn't falling apart around them, but did need a good cleaning. She had a baby who might disrupt everything. And they were attracted to each other.

But he also had a business he was trying to buy. In their phone interview he'd told her he needed to be in West Virginia to be close to the seller. And now he needed somebody who could bring order to the chaos of this house.

"Maybe I *should* ask for more money?" Cheeky, perhaps even a tad over-confident, she strolled over to him. "You're stuck here. There is no cleaning service in Towering Pines. You're also lucky you found me—an administrative assistant who doesn't mind a temporary job and has time to work at your beck and call. You have what? Four weeks to negotiate this deal before Jimmy Lane loses interest and moves on?" She smiled. "I think you're the one who isn't in a position to negotiate."

He held her gaze. "So you're saying it wouldn't cause a problem for you if I asked you to clean this kitchen while I left for a conference call?"

"Are you going to give me the raise?"

"How much?"

"Another two thousand."

His eyes narrowed, but they never left hers. "All right. But you'd better be worth it."

She strolled away, suddenly seeing that the best way to communicate with this man was as an equal. And maybe that was what Brody was doing wrong? Not quite sure where that thought had come from, she shook her head to dislodge it and went back to the negotiations at hand.

"Sure. I'll clean in between administrative assistant

assignments. As long as you don't mind that I wear old jeans and ugly sweatshirts."

He crossed his arms on his chest. "Look around. There's nobody here to impress. And even if there were this house would ruin any chance we had of impressing them."

She couldn't help it. She laughed. "Yeah. Big-time."

"So we have a deal? You work as my administrative assistant when I need you and clean in your downtime. You can dress any way you want and bring your baby." He caught her gaze again. "As long as you keep her out of my way."

"Does 'out of your way' mean you don't want to see her? Because I was hoping I could keep her in the same room with me. I have a swing that will rock her to sleep and keep her sleeping for hours."

He groaned and squeezed his eyes shut, but in the end he sighed and said, "Fine. But if she cries you leave the room."

"Got it."

"Great. As long as we stick to our commitments, this should work out fine." He walked over and held out his hand to shake on the deal.

When Gwen took it, little sparkles of awareness danced up her arm. Their gazes caught and clung.

Now all they had to do was forget about their attraction.

CHAPTER THREE

DREW turned to leave the room, his hand tingling from just touching Gwen's. He told himself it was ridiculous to be attracted to somebody closer to Brody's age than his own—and with a *baby,* no less—but it didn't stop the tightness that had captured his chest.

"Um, Drew?"

He stopped. Half afraid she was about to say something about their attraction—maybe even tell him she didn't want her *old* boss hitting on her—he faced her.

"We still need supplies." She winced. "I brought my equipment from home, but no real cleaning supplies. To make the bathrooms usable I think we need some disinfectant cleanser." She caught his gaze. "I also noticed there are no sheets or towels or pillows. No laundry detergent, dishwashing detergent, dishes or silverware. Or even basic pots and pans. You could also probably use a coffee-maker—"

Relieved that she was focusing on the job, Drew reached for his wallet. "And food?"

"And food."

"Okay." He pulled out several hundred-dollar bills. "Can you take care of getting all of that?"

"I don't think we have a choice."

She glanced at the stack of bills then back up at him. "You

do realize we don't have a Saks Fifth Avenue, right? I'm only going to the local discount department store."

"Are you telling me you have too much money or not enough?"

"I'm saying the sheets won't be silk."

He laughed.

A wonderful feeling filled her again. Her pulse scrambled. Her knees weakened. Her brain became fuzzy and dreamy. When he wasn't being angry with Brody, he was actually a fun, nice guy—

That had to be irrelevant! It would be insanity for a woman with a baby to find a man who obviously didn't like kids attractive. Especially a boss. A rich boss. A man so far out of her league she shouldn't even be looking at him.

Drew's cell phone rang in the silent kitchen. He clicked a button and said, "Teaberry." A pause. "Actually, I don't even have my laptop set up yet. The fax, printer and two boxes of files are still in my SUV."

He walked toward the kitchen door. "I pretty much know Jimmy Lane's biggest objection to the Teaberry Corporation buying his company is that I'm not a local, but I'm fixing that. I'm moving into my grandparents' old homestead," he said, shoving against the swinging door and then disappearing behind it, effectively shutting off his conversation to her.

Ignoring the unwanted sparkle still twinkling through her, Gwen glanced down at sleeping Claire. "Well, this is going to be different than what we'd expected, but not something we can't handle."

Once Claire was dressed in her snowsuit, Gwen left for the store. A few more inches of fresh snow had fallen on the road since her last trip, making the drive down the mountain slow. She spent an hour at the discount department store, and another hour at the grocery, trying to guess what two rich guys would be able to cook for breakfast, lunch and dinner.

With her shopping completed, she stopped at her house. Not only did she pack extra clothes for Claire, she packed extra clothes for herself. She'd leave at least two outfits of cleaning clothes and two outfits of administrative assistant clothes in the maid's quarters, just in case.

She also packed Claire's swing—a gift she'd gotten at her baby shower. Now she had Drew's full permission to have Claire at the house, there was no reason Claire couldn't be totally comfortable.

The drive back up the mountain was even slower than the drive down. When she entered the kitchen, carrying Claire in the baby carrier and three plastic bags of towels, Brody was sitting at the kitchen table, looking bored out of his mind.

"Help me bring in the things from my car, would you?" she said lightly as she dropped the bags on the kitchen floor. She tossed her keys to Brody. "I'll be out in two minutes. I just need to put Claire down for her nap."

She didn't know where Drew was, but she and Brody took so long carrying in the bags and putting the groceries into the kitchen pantry that Claire had awakened from her nap. After Gwen got Claire from the bedroom and fed her, she again found Brody in the kitchen.

"Blue towels and linens are yours," she said to Brody, who was remarkably cooperative. From the way he'd behaved with his father, she'd thought he'd throw a fit when she asked for his help. But he hadn't even flinched when she'd asked him to carry in the groceries and linens. She pointed at the bags that contained his linens. "Why don't you take them upstairs?"

He grabbed the bags. "Got it." He turned to leave the kitchen, but as he passed the table where Claire sat in her carrier he stopped and smiled at the baby. "She's cute."

"Yeah." Gwen smiled, too. Another surprise. She'd have thought rich, obviously spoiled Brody wouldn't care one way or another for a baby. "I adore her."

The swinging door opened and Drew walked in. "Hey." He glanced at the bags still on the floor and the cleaning supplies lined up on the kitchen counter and faced Gwen. "Thanks."

Brody turned away from Claire. Without a word, he headed out of the room.

Drew winced, but swung his gaze to Gwen. "I didn't expect you back so soon."

"I've been gone for hours."

"Really?" He looked at his watch. "Wow. That time certainly flew."

The temptation to remind him that he'd left Brody alone and bored the whole time she was gone was strong, but she resisted. Not only had he scoffed when she'd suggested she might be able to help with his son, but also he hadn't added "help with his son" to the list of things he wanted her to do when they were negotiating. It might not have been intentional, but Brody was his child. His responsibility. She was only an employee. If he wanted her help, he'd have to ask for it.

Still, she couldn't resist the urge to mention that Brody had carried in the bags—if only because the way Brody behaved had her thinking something was off in the relationship between Drew and his son. Maybe even unjustly off.

"Brody carried in most of the groceries and linens. I couldn't have done it without him."

He sighed. "Yeah, I figured that out. His mother's never complained about him. Deep down he's an okay kid. I'm getting the feeling he's just mad at me."

Drew's cell phone rang again.

He clicked the button. "Teaberry. Can you hold on a second,

Hal?" He caught Gwen's gaze. "Two things. First, while you were gone I got a lot of the dust up in the office."

Her eyes widened in surprise. She couldn't imagine a man in a pale blue cashmere sweater dusting a filthy room, but now that he mentioned it she did see a fine coating of dust on his sweater and jeans.

"So I'm ready to start working. I'm going to have a list of people I want you to e-mail with the landline number for the phone. But while I'm gathering that list of names why don't you go check on Brody? Maybe take the vacuum cleaner upstairs and show him how to use it. I'd do it, but I have a feeling he'll listen better to you."

Gwen's heart turned over in her chest. Brody was a good kid, and Drew seemed like an okay guy, yet the two of them seemed to be at war. Still, she'd pushed her luck already, getting to keep this job. She wouldn't overstep any boundaries.

Tuesday morning she came prepared. Revved up. Ready to go. With a sloppy sweatshirt and jeans under her thick coat, she let herself into the kitchen and found Brody at the stove, making eggs—which were burning.

Choking as she entered the room, she used her free hand to wave the smoke around. "Step away from the stove."

He laughed. "My pleasure."

She set Claire's carrier on the table and immediately took the skillet off the gas burner. Before she could do anything else Drew burst into the room. "I'm getting e-mails from three lawyers, all of whom have looked at a different part of the agreement I want to send to Jimmy Lane. I need you in the office now!"

As quickly as he'd popped into the room he popped back out. Gwen glanced at the baby carrier, then at Brody.

He said, "Go. I'll make toast. I'm fine."

She quickly grabbed the baby carrier, put sleepy Claire into the portable crib, stashed the baby monitor in the big pocket in front of her sweatshirt and raced to the office. When she got there, Drew was on the phone. After two minutes of listening to him argue with an attorney, she glanced longingly at the door.

She could have made Brody's eggs by now. Maybe even the toast.

After five minutes she started to fume. She could have easily made Brody's eggs, put on a pot of coffee, squeezed some orange juice *and* set up Claire's swing in the office.

Just when she was ready to leave to do something productive, Drew ended his phone call.

"Okay. I've e-mailed all three lawyers' comments on the agreement to the account I set up for you. All you have to do is print them."

She opened her mouth to lambast him for calling her in for such a simple assignment and then making her wait, but he added, "Your password is Claire."

Her anger deflated. He'd remembered her baby's name? Stupid, dreamy thoughts about how romantic that was popped into her head. But she stopped them. Mostly because they were ridiculous, schoolgirl stupidity. She wasn't a schoolgirl anymore. She was an adult. A woman with a baby. Someone who didn't build fantasies around offhand comments.

When she was done printing the legal assessments, Drew told her to clean the master bedroom. He pointed at the sofa. "I slept on that last night and it wasn't even a little comfortable."

She caught the giggle that nearly bubbled out. It wasn't funny that he'd been uncomfortable, but the look on his handsome face was priceless. Still, she only nodded her understanding and left the room.

She ran into Brody on the way to the maid's quarters to check on Claire before she went upstairs.

"What's up?"

"Nothing." She stopped in front of him. "I'm just on my way to clean the master suite."

"Need any help?"

She swallowed her surprise. "Well, yes and no. I am capable of cleaning that room myself. But a little help would make the job go faster."

"I'll get the vacuum."

The master suite was huge, but as dirty as everything else. While Brody sucked dust off the heavy drapes, the bare mattress, the walls and the carpeting, Gwen cleaned the bathroom. Brody put the sheets and pillows on the big bed. She placed towels in the bathroom. In two hours they had the room sparkling.

Brody said, "Now what?"

She shrugged. "I need to check in with your dad. See what he wants me to do."

His eyes darkened. "Okay."

"Hey, if it's housework, I'll happily share it with you."

"Might as well. There's nothing else to do in this dump."

With that Brody left the room, and Gwen stared after him. When he was busy he didn't call the place a dump. One word from her to Drew could get Brody something to do. But she was so afraid to say that word. She'd already pushed him by negotiating to keep Claire in his house, and she'd pushed it even further by demanding extra money for helping with the cleaning.

And Brody was his son. That was personal. She couldn't, absolutely couldn't, butt into that.

Unfortunately, when she reached Drew's office and he kept her waiting as he talked on the phone for forty-five minutes, stopping her every time she headed for the door, with a "just one more minute" signal with his index finger, she truly empathized with Brody's boredom.

In fact she'd got so bored by the time he disconnected his call that she said, "You do realize Brody is bored, right?"

His face scrunched in confusion. "What?"

"While you're back here working, Brody's rambling around this big house with nothing to do."

Obviously impatient, Drew glanced down at the notes he'd taken during his phone conversation.

Irritation crackled through her. "Don't you care?"

Drew looked up slowly, hooked her gaze and held it for several seconds without saying a word. Finally, he said, "He has a cell phone that connects him to his friends and probably hundreds of thousands of online games. He's fine. This is none of your business."

Because he had her on that, she answered honestly. "Maybe not. But I'm the one walking around the house, bumping into him, seeing how bored he is, and you're the one sitting back here so engrossed in your work that I'll bet you don't even know what time it is."

As if to confirm her suspicion, Drew's gaze fell to the clock on his desk. His face registered shock, but his voice was calm when he said, "Since it troubles you so much, you'll be glad to know I talked with Max, the farm's caretaker, this morning. I want to open up the Christmas tree farm, and he tells me that with a little help he could probably be ready Saturday after next. Once Max gets here this afternoon Brody's going to have plenty to do."

Her mouth fell open in dismay. She didn't know which part of his plan to address first. "You're going to make him work on the Christmas tree farm?"

Drew glanced up lazily. "I take it you have a problem with that, too?"

Embarrassment suffused her. Was she an idiot? Arguing with the man who literally held her future in his hands? The salary from this job would make it possible for her to finish her education, and once she finished her education she could get a teaching job to support herself and Claire. They wouldn't live in the lap of luxury, but they'd be fine. Especially since she and Gill had inherited her mom's house in Towering Pines. Gill didn't want it, but to Gwen it was home. Not having to pay rent meant she really could live comfortably.

If she got her degree.

Suddenly Claire's cry roared through the baby monitor in her sweatshirt pocket. Drew about jumped out of his seat. "What was that?"

She pulled the monitor from her pocket. "Baby monitor. Claire's awake." Without another word, she headed out of the office.

He stopped her. "I'm going to need an hour or two to review some new information I just got. It would be great if you could clean the kitchen."

"Okay." Great. That kept her and Claire out of his way, and gave her something to do—but not Brody. Of course, if he strolled into the kitchen again she could ask him to help her, but by now she was feeling like his taskmaster. Brody had already volunteered more than the normal sixteen-year-old. What he needed was something fun to do. Like snowboarding or skiing.

After changing and feeding Claire, Gwen set up the baby swing in the kitchen and started cleaning. Either Drew or Brody had cleaned enough that they could use the stove, sink, countertops and table. So she dusted the walls, wiped down the cabinets and scrubbed the floor.

When Drew arrived in the kitchen two hours later he looked around in amazement. "Wow. This place is actually nice."

Glad that he wasn't angry with her for her interference about Brody that morning, she panted in a breath and straightened up from the mop. "Cleaning doesn't have to take long."

"Yeah, but I don't think I could have made it look this good this quickly."

His unexpected praise filled her with warmth. But she reminded herself that he was her boss and he was supposed to praise good work. He hadn't told her she was pretty or sweet. He appreciated the work she was doing in his house. There was nothing more to the compliment than that. Besides, she probably looked like something the cat brought in after sweating over the dirty walls and cabinets.

"I'm making a sandwich for lunch. Care to join me?"

"Sure." She glanced at Claire, who had tired herself out in her swing and was ready to nod off. "But first I need to take Claire back to the bedroom for a nap."

She warmed a bottle while Drew gathered cold cuts and condiments from the refrigerator. When the bottle was ready, she slid Claire out of the swing and headed for the bedroom. Claire ate greedily and immediately fell asleep. Gwen returned to the kitchen and found Drew sitting alone at the table.

"Where's Brody?"

He finished the last bite of the sandwich on his plate, then said, "I called him. He should be here soon."

Brody slogged into the kitchen and flopped into a chair. Not wanting an argument to ensue, Gwen quickly prepared a sandwich for him and brought him a glass of milk.

Drew made himself another sandwich and took the seat beside Brody. Wanting everything to go well, Gwen poured some potato chips into a bowl and set them on the table, along with a bag of store-bought cookies.

As she sat, Drew said, "Gwen tells me you have nothing to do."

Her eyes widened and she gaped at him, but before she could say anything, he continued, "I know it's boring here. My dad told me stories about being so bored here before your grandfather moved to North Carolina that he thought he'd go nuts. So I've arranged for something to do for you."

Brightening, Brody sat up.

Gwen's chest tightened with fear. She might not have been a parent long, but she absolutely knew Drew was going about this all the wrong way.

"We're opening up the Christmas tree farm."

Brody said, "What?"

"The farm. We're opening it. Jimmy Lane used to come to Teaberry Farms for his tree when he was a young father. He's eager to see the place again. I thought it would be good for him if it was up and running. Sort of recreate that memory for him."

Brody just gaped at his dad.

Drew obliviously trotted on. "Max is coming over this afternoon to start harvesting the trees. He's already investigated how we should price them. We'll have bunches of pre-cut trees for people in a hurry, and let other people go into the fields to choose their own. It will be fun."

Brody's gape turned into a look of utter horror. *"Fun?"*

"Sure."

"And how much of this fun are *you* going to have?"

"Hey, I'll be plenty busy."

"Yeah," Brody said, shoving back his chair as he rose. "Inside. In your warm office. While I'm outside freezing and lugging trees."

"Brody, you know I have to work—"

"Right. Work. That's all you think about. You didn't really

come up with the Christmas tree farm idea for me. You need the farm open to impress the old guy, and you're using me as slave labor."

"That's not how it is!"

"Uh-huh? Sure. First Mom doesn't want me because she's got a new life, a new husband—" Brody's voice shook, and Gwen's heart squeezed with empathy for his pain. "Now you're using me to get a business deal."

He turned and strode to the back door, where he plucked his parka from a hook by the door.

Drew rose. "Brody, wait! Stop! I'm not using you for slave labor! And your mother isn't abandoning you just because she got married."

When Brody turned to face them, tears glistened on his eyelids. "Oh, that's right. She probably hasn't called you yet. But she will. I heard her telling Marc that she'd 'take care of it' after they got back from their honeymoon. She says you can't argue about keeping me now, since she's had me my whole life and you've barely seen me. So it's your turn."

With that he stormed out the door. Gwen sat stunned. Drew hovered by the table, obviously shell shocked. "I have absolutely no idea what to do."

She said nothing.

He glanced down. "You offered to give me advice. I need advice. So you can start talking anytime now."

"You scoffed at my advice, remember? And just this morning you told me that Brody was none of my concern."

"Well, I'm not so picky now."

She sucked in a breath. Sixteen-year-old boys didn't cry unless something was seriously wrong—horribly wrong. So wrong he felt totally out of control. But if she told Drew that he wouldn't sensitively delve until he got to the heart of the matter. He'd probably yell, or say something he'd regret, or both. He had to spend enough time with Brody until Brody was comfortable enough to talk or until the answers revealed themselves. And, though she knew Drew would probably groan at her suggestion, she decided to go with it anyway.

She caught his gaze. "Okay. If it were me running out that door right now, feeling like one parent didn't want me and the other was about to turn me into a slave, I'd probably wish for a few minutes alone so my dad didn't see me crying."

Drew sat.

"Then I might feel totally different about the whole slave labor thing if my dad came out and did some of the work."

He mouth dropped open. "You want *me* to help run the Christmas tree farm?"

"Maybe at least do some of the prep work to get it ready for customers?"

"I have a conglomerate to run and I'm in the middle of buying a new company."

"So?"

He gaped at her. "So?"

"So what's more important? Your company or your son?"

CHAPTER FOUR

DREW shrugged into his coat and headed out the door. Gwen had insisted he take Brody's sandwich with him, so he had it in a little plastic bag and felt like a kid on his way to his first day of school.

He found Brody leaning against the SUV. "Here."

He looked at the sandwich, then looked at his dad. "I'm not hungry."

Max Peabody appeared around the other side of the SUV. With his snow-white hair and beard, and rosy-red cheeks, he looked a bit like Santa Claus in jeans.

"You better eat that sandwich, boy! Harvesting Christmas trees will work up a powerful appetite."

Drew nearly groaned in anticipation of the myriad smart remarks Brody would make. But instead, Brody snatched the little baggie from Drew's hand and took out the sandwich.

"Okay. I'm glad that's settled." Max looked around with pleasure at the trees around them. "Like I said on the phone, we can open Saturday after next, but we'll need time to get the place ready. There are tons of old tree branches and debris in the rows between the trees." He winked at Drew. "Don't want a lawsuit because someone trips over a branch."

He glanced around again. "Then we'll need a few days to cut some trees for people who don't want to go out in the field. Which actually works out pretty well, because while we're harvesting I can teach you guys how to cut trees so that you can go out with the customers who want to choose their own." He pointed at a rundown outbuilding. "There's a little stand stored in there. We used it as a checkout table where my wife Sunny used to take the money from customers." He sent his gaze back to Drew. "But if you're trying to impress somebody, we're probably going to have to spruce up these old outbuildings. It's too cold and wet to paint them, but it wouldn't hurt to replace the missing boards."

Brody glanced fearfully at Drew. Drew tried his damnedest to smile. He saw himself putting in eight-hour days on the farm and then eight hours in the office at night. And all of this was Gwen's fault.

The second he thought of her his blood heated. She held her ground with him like no one else in his world had ever even tried. And she was cute about it. Her nose wrinkled. Her eyes sparked with fire. He couldn't even imagine what kind of liberties she'd take with him if he wasn't her boss and she spoke freely.

His heart-rate spiked and the temperature of his blood rose another degree or two. He didn't know whether to laugh or groan. Thinking about her might be a way to keep from freezing to death while lugging trees in this frozen tundra of a farm. But thinking about her all afternoon while he tromped around might make it a little harder to be a good, objective boss when he came back inside to work at night.

Because they *would* be working together at night.

That would be her punishment for coming up with this hare-brained scheme. Opening the Christmas tree farm might have been his idea, but his sharing the labor had been hers. So she would suffer right along with him.

* * *

Gwen watched out the kitchen window as Max waved his hands around in the general direction of the vast expanse of trees beyond them. She saw Brody eating the sandwich she'd sent out and sighed with relief. But her sigh was short-lived when she saw Drew cast a narrow-eyed look in the direction of the house.

She dropped the curtain and jumped back from the window. Oh, he was going to make her pay for this.

Deciding the best defense was a good offense, Gwen took the roast she'd bought when she was at the grocery store the day before, cut it into cubes, and began preparing a hearty stew. She peeled potatoes and carrots, browned the meat, and made a rich gravy. When everything was on the burner to simmer, a thought occurred to her, and she went in search of the things she'd need to make homemade dinner rolls.

Once the dough was rising, she decided to also make home-made muffins. It was one of the skills her mom had taught her. She and Gill loved muffins, so at a very young age Ginger had shown her girls how to make their own.

By the time Drew and Brody stomped into the house five hours later the stew bubbled on the stove, fresh dinner rolls sat in a basket and the sweet scent of pumpkin muffins permeated the air.

Drew dropped his gloves on the counter and sniffed. "This has to be heaven."

"Anywhere would be heaven compared to that damn field."

Drew bit back a sigh. Brody hadn't really complained all day, for which Drew thanked God, but now that they were away from Max his son was back to saying damn and would probably be snotty for the rest of the night.

Deciding that ignoring Brody might be the thing to do, he focused on the obvious. "Everything smells great." Because that was the absolute truth, he closed his eyes in ecstasy. "I only hope I have the strength to eat it."

Brody snorted a laugh and headed for the swinging door. "I want to clean up."

When he was gone, Drew caught Gwen's gaze. All day long he'd thought about ways he'd punish her for her idea, but now that he had her alone, in a kitchen that smelled so good he could have eaten the table, he was suddenly tongue-tied.

"These are just a few things my mom taught me to make."

"Your mom must be an excellent cook."

"She was."

"Was?"

"She passed away. It was a year last September."

"I'm sorry."

She shrugged and grabbed plates from the cupboard. "It's okay. Gill and I have each other."

Feeling awkward about having her wait on him, Drew headed for the silverware drawer. "Gill is your sister?"

"Twin sister."

He stopped. Smiled stupidly. "You're a twin?"

"It doesn't make me a freak."

"No. I think it's kind of cute." He did. Damn it. Everything he heard about her made her special. And she'd fixed them dinner. She hadn't rested on her laurels while he was outside. She'd done the thing that most needed to be done: she'd made food, probably recognizing that they'd be starving.

They ate dinner in near silence. Not because they were tiptoeing around each other, but because the men didn't pause long enough between bites of food to converse. After he'd eaten Brody excused himself. Drew knew he was going upstairs to bed. He didn't stop him. Drew would have liked to drop into a warm bed himself right now. But everything he'd neglected while learning to cut and prune Christmas trees now had to be addressed.

"You *do* know we'll have to work tonight, right?"

She nodded. "Yes." She caught his gaze. "You *do* know that I'll have to have Claire in the office in her swing, right?"

"Yes."

"So we're set?"

He couldn't help it. He smiled at her. She didn't leave anything to chance, but more than that she negotiated with him like an equal. She wasn't afraid of anything. Not even him. She had so much spunk and intelligence that if she didn't live so far away from North Carolina he'd probably hire her for his corporate office.

Of course then he'd have to deal with being attracted to her and not being allowed to kiss her or touch her or sleep with her—

Sleep with her? Oh, Lord. Why had he let *that* thought form? The vision of having her warm and naked beside him shot an arrow of arousal through him. The images in his brain weren't just crystal-clear, they came with feelings that rumbled through him. *Feelings.* His attraction was morphing into something he didn't dare even name—because he didn't want it and neither should she.

He bounced from his seat. "Let's get to work."

They worked until ten. At ten, tired from his manual labor, Drew ran his hand down his face and said, "That's it. I'm done for the night."

She collapsed on her desk. "I'm so glad you said that."

He laughed. "Go home."

She immediately rose. "You don't have to tell me twice."

With that she left the room, and Drew chuckled again then caught himself. He liked her too much. Everything about her. He wasn't just attracted to her because she was gorgeous. She had given him good advice about Brody, had cooked a great supper, and hadn't complained when he'd told her she'd have to work late.

He rose from the desk and ambled into the kitchen, where he grabbed one of her homemade muffins and groaned in ecstasy when he bit into it. She really was too good to be true. *And too young for him.* He had to remember that. She was young and smart and had her whole life in front of her. What the hell would she want with a guy twelve years older than she was?

After finishing his muffin, he headed down the hall to the foyer stairs. Unfortunately, when he rounded the corner, he nearly bumped into Gwen. He skidded to a stop. So did she.

"Sorry," automatically came out of his mouth, then his gaze collided with her baby carrier and he took a step back. "I forgot all about Claire. I thought you said she'd have to be in the office with us?"

She shrugged. "She was asleep when I got done with the kitchen so I let her sleep on." She laughed lightly. "I told you she was a good baby."

"Yes." But it was cold outside. Bitter cold. And not only had Gwen bundled herself to go home, but she'd had to bundle her baby. Now she'd drive fifteen or twenty minutes in the cold to get into town and to her house.

The urge to tell her to stay the night rose up in him like a tsunami. But when he met the gaze of her pretty green eyes his stomach plummeted. Damn, she was gorgeous. And he *was* attracted to her. If he asked her to stay, she might take it the wrong way. Worse, she might take it the right way and agree that sleeping at his house was smarter and safer. Then he'd probably lie in his bed thinking about how she was downstairs. How he was attracted to her and how he couldn't have her. And he wouldn't get any sleep.

Reminding himself that the roads were safe and she was a West Virginia girl, accustomed to driving in the snow, he reached for the doorknob and opened the door for her. "See you tomorrow."

She smiled her beautiful smile at him. "See you tomorrow."

She walked out into the cold, and as he watched her go he noticed the little puff of smoke coming from the exhaust pipe of her car. She'd already started it. At least he didn't have to worry about her and the baby being cold on the drive down.

When she was gone, he sucked in a breath.

It had been one hell of a two days. First he couldn't deal with Brody. Then he was attracted to the woman he'd hired to be his assistant, and if that wasn't bad enough she had a baby. Then he had to do manual labor to make his son feel he wasn't a slave. And now he couldn't even do the kindness of letting his secretary and her baby stay at his house because he was worried about his attraction to her.

Somehow, some way, he had to get control of something.

Gwen had breakfast ready when Brody and Drew woke up the next morning. She'd warmed the pumpkin muffins in the oven and made fresh coffee, eggs and bacon. She knew the scent of it greeted them as they pushed inside through the swinging door.

"I'm famished," Brody said without preamble.

Drew's gaze met hers. "Me, too."

She smiled to hide the shiver that raced through her. From the way he'd looked at her the night before when she left, she knew that he might be hungry for food, but he also felt something for her. Probably the same crazy thing that rose up in her every time she looked at him.

But she'd already sorted this out in her head. He was too

old for her. He came from a different world than she did. A world she probably wouldn't fit in because she loved her small town. Plus, she had a baby. He didn't like babies, and even if he did she and Claire couldn't possibly fit into his life when Brody barely did.

That settled in her head once again, she joined the men when they sat at the table.

Drew peeked at her. "What time did you have to get up to be here and have all this ready by seven o'clock in the morning?"

"Four." She laughed. "But don't worry. Some days Claire gets me up at four. The days she doesn't want to go back to sleep, I'm happy to have something to do rather than sit in my dark living room."

The look he gave her tightened her chest. She wasn't sure what was going on in his brain, but something about her getting up in the middle of the night didn't sit well with him.

Before she could say anything, Max arrived. "Ready to work?"

Both men groaned. When they did, Gwen noticed the strange look Brody gave his dad. It seemed Drew had won Brody's respect—not by being willing to work alongside him, but by hating the work as much as Brody did.

Drew rose. "Do you have things to do today?" he asked Gwen as he walked to the hooks by the back door to retrieve his coat.

"Plenty," Gwen assured him.

He sucked in a breath, caught her gaze and said, "Then we're off."

Brody slapped him on the shoulder. "Don't worry, Dad. You'll get the hang of that saw eventually."

With that they left, and Gwen stared at the door smiling.

Brody had spoken normally to his dad. And he'd slapped his shoulder affectionately.

She really had given Drew the right advice.

Lunch was quickly eaten sandwiches, but when the Teaberry men stepped into the house for supper the scent of gingerbread greeted them.

Drew saw a baked chicken, mashed potatoes, stuffing and green beans all sitting on the stove waiting for them, but the gingerbread stole his attention.

"Did you make real gingerbread men? From scratch?"

"Yes. They're one of my favorites."

He met her gaze. A warm, syrupy feeling flooded him. He now understood how men in the old west had felt when they'd come home to a log cabin that smelled like supper. "They're my favorites, too."

She smiled. "Thanks. I really love to cook."

And he really loved to eat. He nearly sighed. They complemented each other so well that it seemed impossible they weren't allowed to have a relationship.

"Hey, I like gingerbread men, too," Brody said, grabbing one and stuffing it into his mouth. "Umm. They *are* good."

Gwen playfully slapped his hand. "You're going to spoil your dinner."

"No worry on that," Drew answered for Brody. "Max worked us so hard today we'll probably each need two dinners."

She laughed and told them to wash up. They left the kitchen, and when they entered the hall Drew saw rows of gold tinsel strung along the now clean walls. They spiraled up the banister of the stairway. Red bows with bright red and gold Christmas tree ornaments accented the tinsel.

Brody glanced around in awe. "Wow!"

Drew looked around, too. "Yeah, wow. I can't believe she did all this and made dinner."

Brody said, "I can't believe how cool this looks."

Drew peered at him. "Seriously?"

"Yeah. It's great."

Drew thought his son a little too old to be awed by a bit of tinsel, but he didn't mention that. He had noticed the calluses forming on Brody's hands, because he had corresponding calluses on his own hands, but that moment of camaraderie there in the foyer, looking at the Christmas decorations, made it all worth it. Two days ago Brody would have stormed by the decorations. He wouldn't have spoken to his dad. Today they'd talked like normal guys. A father and son.

Gwen had been right. Working together was changing Brody. Relaxing him. Bringing back the son Drew remembered.

They returned to the kitchen and Brody complimented Gwen profusely on the decorations. "My mom doesn't do anything like this," he said, then dug into his chicken with gusto. "She has these weird blue and pink decorations that don't look like Christmas at all. But these," he said, pointing at the hallway, "look like the things we had in elementary school. That was when Christmas really felt like Christmas."

Drew glanced up at Gwen, who nodded her head slightly in acknowledgement of the silent thanks he'd sent. He'd never thought of his son as deprived, and he certainly wasn't. But it was sad that his favorite Christmas memories were from so long ago. Maybe that was his fault? Maybe it was Brody's mom's? Maybe it was life changing as Brody grew older? But whatever the reason it troubled Drew that Brody believed his best Christmases were a decade behind him.

Fierce fatherly instinct rose up in him. He had three weeks

until Christmas, and somehow, some way, he wanted to make this a Christmas Brody would never forget.

The only problem was...he wasn't sure how.

CHAPTER FIVE

THE next week, Drew and Brody worked feverishly with Max, removing the last of the debris and cutting trees for customers. But on the Friday before opening day Max called to let them know he couldn't come over until the afternoon because his wife Sunny had a doctor's appointment. After a hearty breakfast, Drew and Brody headed for the door.

"Max told us we'd need to replace the missing boards on the old shed," Drew explained to Gwen as they slid into their outdoor gear. "I think we can handle that on our own."

"Sure, and why not set up the stand, too?" Brody groused. "It's not like a morning off after nearly two weeks of slave labor would have been a good idea."

Seeing the look of confusion that came to Drew's handsome face, Gwen felt her chest swell with fear. He and his son had been getting along so well that it surprised her that Brody picked this morning to return to being a brat. She suspected Max probably acted like a buffer or referee for them, and worried that after two wonderful weeks of comradeship they'd get into a deal-breaker fight without someone to run interference.

Still, Drew headed to the door and Brody followed him outside. Then they were gone. Out of her sight. There was nothing she could do now about what happened between them.

Fear scuttled through her again, and she knew she had to keep herself busy or she'd fret all morning.

She carted Claire and her baby swing into the living room. Though she'd vacuumed the furniture, walls and carpet of every room to get up the dust, this room had fallen to a place close to the bottom on the "real" cleaning list. Only the formal dining room and guest bedrooms were below it. But today was the day she had to dig in.

She vacuumed everything again, getting any stubborn dust that might have resisted during her initial vacuum, and then washed the windows, walls and woodwork. When the room was clean she glanced around. She'd brought the tinsel and ribbons and ornaments from home to decorate the hallway and make sure Jimmy Lane walked into a pretty entrance in case he made a surprise visit. But now that the room was clean, the fireplace screamed for some tinsel. Maybe stockings, too?

She'd only brought enough decorations for the hallway, and didn't have anything else at home she could spare. So she headed for the attic. People who didn't take their furniture usually also left behind the contents of attics and basements. Maybe she'd find some decorations there?

She went upstairs and found a virtual treasure trove. Sealed from the dust and grime of the attic in airtight boxes, the ornaments, lights, tinsel, stockings and Christmas tree star she found were like new. She carted them downstairs, but before she set about decorating she knew she had to put Claire down for a nap.

In the kitchen, making Claire's bottle, she saw the milk in the fridge and another idea struck her. She'd worried all morning about Drew and Brody, and it was only eleven o'clock. They'd be out there at least another hour before she'd get to see how they'd gotten along without Max. But if she took hot cocoa out to them she could not only give them a break, she could also see if they were fighting.

She fed Claire, put her down for her nap, made the chocolate and, as casually as she could, took a Thermos of hot cocoa and paper cups outside. Not seeing Drew or Brody anywhere, she peeked into the shed and there they were—standing over some boards so old they were black.

"I think we should carry these boards outside and rebuild the shed out there, rather than rebuild it in here and have to lug it outside."

Brody leaned negligently against a beam. "Whatever."

"Come on, Brody. We open tomorrow. We don't have time for this."

Deciding that this was a great moment to interrupt them, Gwen stepped into the shed. "Hey! How's it going? I brought hot chocolate."

Brody glanced gratefully in her direction. Drew slid off his gloves before he took the Thermos from her hands. "Great. I'm dying of thirst."

"Yeah, and it's not like the house isn't thirty feet away and we could stop for water or anything."

"If you're thirsty, all you have to do is go in the house and get a drink—"

"And get the third degree about why I'm leaving?"

Knowing that a real argument was about to ensue, Gwen pointed at the old steel-runner sled hanging on the wall and quickly said, "Hey, look! It's an old sled."

Her comment was just confusing enough to stop the men. Both glanced in the direction she pointed.

Drew smiled. "I haven't seen one of those in ages."

Gwen turned to Brody. "Do you sled-ride?"

"I snowboard and ski."

"You would love an old-fashioned sled ride," she said, then

faced Drew. "Why don't you two take ten minutes and see if that old thing still works?"

Drew looked at Brody. Brody looked at Drew.

Drew shrugged. "We have to get this shed put together, but we could do that this afternoon, before we go out into the field with Max to cut the last of the trees we'll need for tomorrow."

Brody's eyes lit. "Really? We're going to take a break?"

"Until this afternoon when Max gets here." He pointed at the sled. "Pull that down. We'll see if it works."

Brody lifted the sled from the rack on the wall.

Drew opened the door for him as he carried it outside. "My dad told me stories about a hill behind the house where he rode a sled—probably this one. Let's walk back there and see if we can test it out."

Gwen merrily followed them. Baby monitor in her pocket, she knew she'd hear Claire if she awoke. Plus, they weren't going too far from the house. She could watch Brody and Drew sled-ride for a few minutes before she had to get back inside to start lunch.

They walked only twenty feet or so past the house before Brody stopped suddenly. "Whoa!"

Drew stopped, too. His laugh echoed down the mountain. "That's a hill!"

Brody grabbed the sled. "Me first."

"Absolutely," Drew said. "You be the guinea pig."

Brody laughed, threw the sled down and landed on top of it, sending it careening down the slope. His laughter echoed up to Gwen and Drew, who stood side-by-side at the top of the hill.

When Brody reached the bottom and began carrying the sled back Drew turned to Gwen. "Give me the baby monitor and you can go next."

She stepped back. "That's okay. I don't want a ride."

"Sure you do. I heard you laughing at Brody's fun."

She took another step back. "I know, but I'm kind of scared."

"Scared? Haven't you ever done this before?"

"When I was ten or twelve. But not lately."

"It's fun," Brody said, cresting the hill, obviously having heard their conversation. He offered the sled to her. "Go ahead."

She shook her head fiercely.

Drew took the sled from Brody with one hand and caught her hand with the other. Before she knew what he was about to do, she was pushed down on the sled and Drew landed heavily on top of her. She didn't even have time to squeak out a protest. With the extra weight, the sled didn't fly down the hill the way it had with only Brody on top. Instead, it careered drunkenly. When they hit the bottom, it tilted. Drew rolled off and Gwen rolled on top of him, the breath knocked out of her.

She sucked in some air, then some more, then suddenly realized she was on top of Drew. He blinked up at her. She stared down at him. In that moment they weren't a boss and his assistant. He wasn't old. She wasn't young. They were just two people. Two people incredibly attracted to each other.

The air suddenly became heavy with promise. All she had to do would be to let her head fall a bit and she could kiss him. All he had to do would be to slide his hand a fraction of an inch and he could be touching her bottom.

"Hey! You guys aren't hurt, are you?" Brody's voice got closer with every word, and Gwen realized he was running down the hill. His boots stopped beside her and she raised her gaze to look at him.

"We're fine." But her voice came out as a croak. She'd been

fighting this thing with Drew ever since she first saw him. He was too good-looking. Any woman would find him attractive. But lying on top of him as she was had somehow made it all real. Everything that had seemed vague and dreamlike about considering a relationship with him suddenly felt real.

Possible.

Brody held his hand out to her. "Here."

She glanced at Drew. Their eyes locked. And it didn't take a genius to know his thoughts had gone in the same direction hers had. *That* was why it all suddenly felt possible. They weren't merely attracted, they were becoming friends. Sort of. When they weren't arguing or negotiating.

Realizing she had lingered a little too long, she took Brody's hand. He hoisted her up and she brushed the snow off her jacket and jeans. Then she checked the baby monitor, breathing a sigh of relief when it was not only in one piece, but also silent.

She waved the monitor at the Teaberrys. "I better go check on Claire."

She didn't even wait to see Drew's reaction. She simply headed up the hill, walked into the house, checked on her sleeping baby and started lunch.

She refused to think about the possibility she'd felt at the bottom of that snowy hill. Though she did laugh. Damned if he hadn't gotten her on the sled.

She made lunch—soup and sandwiches—but didn't eat with the Teaberrys. As they laughed and talked about sledding, tingles of awareness pirouetted through her, so she excused herself and went back to work on decorating the living room. She liked Drew. She liked him a lot. Yes, they had their differences, but in some ways that was what made their relationship interesting.

She groaned in her head. Now she was calling what they

had a *relationship?* She was getting too connected to him and his son, and when they left she was going to be hurt. She remembered very well how it had felt to be left behind by Nick when she'd told him she was pregnant. She remembered the pain. The chest-tightening sadness that the man she'd thought she loved didn't care enough about her to help her through a pregnancy. It had taken six months to get beyond her depression and another three to feel happy again. Did she really want to repeat all that pain when she had a chance to avoid it simply by keeping her distance from her boss?

Determined to forget about Drew, she lost herself in Christmas decorating. Stockings were hung on the marble fireplace mantel. Evergreen bows with red velvet ribbons were strung along the top of the tan brocade drapes that covered the two front windows. Santa and Mrs. Santa figurines were placed on the coffee table between the two green plaid sofas that flanked the fireplace. Elf figurines were scattered around the room, making the place look like Santa's workshop.

She was so engrossed in her work that she didn't hear Drew approach until he said, "Wow."

She spun to face him. "You like it?" Her face reddened when she realized how eager she sounded for his approval. She cleared her throat and toned down her enthusiasm. "I found these decorations upstairs. There are boxes of them."

He stepped into the room. "It's perfect." He glanced around, then pointed at the space in front of the side-by-side windows. "Except I think you need a tree."

She laughed. "Here I am at a Christmas tree farm and I don't have a tree."

He looked over at her. His dark eyes sparked with appreciation and something else. Something deeper. Something that made her tummy shimmy, her pulse scramble, and a wave of heat fall from her head to her toes. The feeling of promise she'd felt lying on top of him at the bottom of the hill returned full force.

"I'll get you one."

She swallowed and nodded, and then he was gone. Gwen collapsed on the sofa. She wasn't really sorry she'd taken cocoa out to him and Brody. She wasn't really sorry she'd suggested they sled-ride. She almost wasn't sorry they'd landed on top of each other at the bottom of a snowy hill.

But she had absolutely no idea how she'd handle the ramifications of any of it.

Drew walked straight through the kitchen, grabbed his coat, and went out into the snowy afternoon. He needed the drop in temperature to cool down. Gwen wasn't just cute and sweet. It was as if she read his mind. Everything he needed to have done, she did. Including decorate for Christmas for his son. If he weren't her boss, he wouldn't be able to resist her.

But he was her boss. He was also twelve years older. And he was a workaholic. And she—

He stopped. Snow fell heavily on his shoulders and caught on his eyelashes as he stood confused in the circular driveway of his family's first home. He really didn't know anything about Gwen. He knew she had a child. He knew she had a twin. She'd helped him with his son, cleaned this mess of a house so he could now live in it, cooked, and acted as his administrative assistant and he knew virtually nothing about her.

Was he selfish or was it self-preservation? After all, it wouldn't be smart for them to get involved. Not only were they wrong for each other, but he was leaving soon. And she would—

Damn. He had no idea what she'd do when he left. When he'd tried to fire her she'd told him she desperately needed this job, but he hadn't thought far enough ahead to realize she might not have a way to make money once he was gone.

A bubble of protectiveness formed in his chest. She'd negotiated a little more money from him than the original salary they'd agreed upon, but when he was gone he had no idea how she'd support herself and Claire.

He shook his head resolutely. He couldn't think about that. She was a smart, savvy adult who would be fine. If he meddled in her life they'd get closer, and he might not be able to pull away when the time came. And that would be a disaster. She was young enough and pretty enough that she'd probably forget about him two weeks after he was gone. And then where would he be? Alone in North Carolina, feeling hopeless and dejected, aching with hurt as he had when Olivia left him.

He headed for the shed, hoping Max had arrived so he could get his mind off Gwen. Instead he passed her beaten-up car, and saw that at least four inches of snow had accumulated since her arrival and the storm was just getting started. She'd be driving down a mountain road in a foot of snow tonight.

The protective bubble in his chest tightened. He had to at least offer her the opportunity to stay nights. If he intended to work her fourteen hours a day he had to for once forget about his own fears and think about hers.

Because Claire had taken an overly long nap that afternoon, Gwen brought her to the supper table that night. As she sat, Drew peered over at her precious baby. He let his gaze linger on the little girl, as if taking in every detail about her, maybe growing accustomed to her. Then he turned his attention to Brody, talking about the stand they'd helped Max rebuild.

Gwen happily let the conversation steer itself totally away from her. After the sled ride, then the look he'd given her over the Christmas tree conversation, she knew they'd be better off ignoring each other.

When dinner was eaten, she got up from the table and started the dishes. Brody excused himself for his room, and as he left for the office Drew reminded her that they again had to work that night.

After the dishes were done, she lifted Claire's carrier and headed off to join him. As she stepped inside the office Drew was deep in concentration, reading a document. She settled Claire in the swing.

"Will she be okay?"

His question startled her, but didn't surprise her. She'd caught him staring at Claire at dinner and knew he wasn't complaining as much as acknowledging that he was okay with her being here.

"As long as she can see me she's fine."

Drew set the contract he was reading back on his desk, scrubbed his hand across his face as if wrestling with himself about something, then said, "That's going to be hard when you get a real job."

She frowned. That was a weird comment. Especially since he'd barely ever asked her anything about herself. Their last discussion about something personal about her had been when she'd told him about Gill.

Still, she couldn't ignore him. "I'm not getting a real job for a while. Once this assignment is over I'm taking the money I earn here and using it to support us while I finish my degree."

He sat forward on his chair. "You're that close?"

She nodded and smiled. It felt good to have a real plan, not just a dream or a hope or a wish. "I got pregnant the next-to-last semester of college. I finished that semester, but not the last. So I have to take some classes, but mostly I'll be student teaching."

His eyes lit. "You're going to be a teacher?"

"Yep. So for the next four months, when I'm not teaching or taking a class, I'll be with Claire. But I'll also be away from her enough that I'm hoping she'll adjust to daycare before she has to be there for eight-hour days."

He smiled. "You have it all thought out."

"I have to. I can't leave anything to chance."

"I guess." He fiddled with the pencil he was holding, then caught her gaze again. "Speaking of chance…is there any chance you'd consider sleeping here at nights?" His face reddened endearingly. "I said that wrong. Everything has changed since I decided to open the Christmas tree farm. You're working eight hours in the house during the day and four hours with me at night." He rubbed his hand along the back of his neck. "I worry about you driving down the mountain."

The warm, fuzzy feeling in the pit of her stomach returned. *He worried about her—*

She stopped her thoughts. To her dreamy schoolgirl side that might seem wonderful, but it wasn't smart for two attracted people who were beginning to care about each other to sleep in the same house. He had to know that as much as she did.

She peered over at him.

He held her gaze. "Okay, since the episode on the sled outed both of us, I think it's time for us to be honest." He paused, sucked in a breath. "We're very attracted to each other."

The air in her chest stuttered. She licked her suddenly dry lips. He was right. Since the fall off the sled neither one of them could pretend indifference. Still, she hadn't expected him to come right out and talk about it.

"But our lives are totally different. I'm not going to start something that I know is wrong. So if you agree to stay nights you'll be perfectly safe with me."

His reassurance should have made her happy. After all, he was right about the drive down the mountain at night. Instead, her heart hurt. Her pride felt wounded. He might be attracted to her, but he absolutely, positively didn't want to be. He'd sent her that message every day in subtle, silent ways. And she'd caught it. That was why she held back her own feelings.

But she still had them, and spending more time with him, no matter how convenient and smart it might be, would only add fuel to the fire. She wasn't just attracted to him anymore. She had real feelings for him, and was getting a little too comfortable in this house.

She looked down, then back up at him. "How about if I think about it?"

He nodded, maybe a little too eagerly, as if happy to have the awkward conversation over. "Okay."

Her heart plummeted. It was one thing to decide herself to keep her distance, quite another to have him come right out and say he didn't want anything to do with her.

CHAPTER SIX

As if Mother Nature wanted Teaberry Farms opening day to be a grand success, the snow stopped the next morning. Gwen arrived at the Teaberry mansion to find Max, Drew and Brody sitting at the kitchen table. Jovial Max laughed like a kid at Christmas, Drew grinned—looking every bit as excited as Max—and Brody pouted.

"The three of us will have our work cut out for us this morning," Max said over the rim of his coffee mug. "It's two weeks till Christmas. People are going to be coming in droves. I think it will work best if two of us assist the customers and one mans the cash register."

Brody snorted derisively. Drew nodded. "I'll take the cash register." He glanced at Gwen, his eyes cool, emotionless, telling her with their lack of expression that she truly was safe with him. "I'm expecting a fax around eleven. If I stay in one place all morning, you'll know where to find me when it comes in."

Turning to get a cup from the cupboard, so he wouldn't see the hurt in her eyes, she said, "Okay."

With that, the men rose from the table. Max and Drew grabbed the coats they stored on the hooks by the kitchen door. Brody had to go upstairs for his. In a silent protest at the work he had to do, he'd stopped leaving his parka by the door, so he could delay going outside while he got it.

Seeing a flicker of apprehension race across Drew's face, Gwen said a silent prayer that everything would go okay, and within seconds the men were outside and the Christmas tree farm was officially open.

Gwen carried Claire's swing into the dining room and went to work. She cleaned first, then began to decorate. She strung lights and tinsel through the arms of the chandelier above the long mahogany table, looped tinsel above the tan brocade drapes, and made a centerpiece of evergreens and Christmas tree ornaments for the table.

She longed to see if Drew and Max had any customers. She knew how much Drew was banking on the Christmas tree farm impressing Jimmy Lane. The old man was dragging his feet in negotiations, ignoring Drew's e-mails, and only corresponding enough that Drew knew he hadn't totally lost the possibility of buying Jimmy's company. So Gwen was too apprehensive to even let herself look out the window at their success or failure. It was ridiculous. Foolish. Caring too much about a man who clearly didn't want her was almost as bad as wishing a man would return to her life the way her mom had. She knew better than this.

When Drew's fax arrived at eleven-thirty, she put on her coat and walked out the front door into total chaos. Cars lined the lane that led to the Teaberry mansion. People milled about the groups of already cut trees that leaned against the wood fence for inspection and purchase. A glance past the outbuildings into the rows of uncut trees showed that even more customers were in the field, choosing their very own special tree.

Not even sure where to look for the cash register, Gwen wove through the customers. She saw Max and Brody first, hoisting trees to car roofs and securing them with twine, or shoving them into the backs of SUVs and pickups.

"They're all here because of the legend," she heard Max telling Brody. "Every year someone who buys one of these trees has a fantastic wish granted."

Brody snorted.

"Scoff if you want to," Max said, "but even though only one person gets a great wish, lots of people get little wishes granted. Family members show up unexpectedly for Christmas dinner, special presents arrive, money finds its way into bank accounts." He tapped Brody's shoulder. "And all because there's magic in our trees."

Brody rolled his eyes. "Right."

"And you've been touching them for two weeks now." Max's eyes twinkled. "Imagine how good of a wish you could be granted if you'd just believe."

Not wanting Brody to scoff again, and ruin Max's holiday cheer, Gwen rushed over to them. "Where's Drew?"

Max pointed to a crowded area. "He's at the back of that line, taking money."

Following the direction of Max's glove-covered finger, Gwen looped around the crowd and saw Drew.

A short woman in a worn blue coat walked up to the sales stand as his next customer. "How much?"

Drew examined her tree as Brody and Max approached. "Thirty… Um…" He looked down at the tattered wallet the woman produced from her coat pocket at the same time as Gwen noticed the big sign behind the makeshift checkout area. The sign said the trees were priced at five dollars a foot, and this customer had at least a six-foot tree.

She didn't expect Drew to realize that thirty dollars was a lot of money. In his world it probably wasn't. But in the world of the woman in the tattered coat it was a small fortune.

He glanced down at the cash register, then looked up with a beaming smile. "Guess what? Your tree is free. You're our one-hundredth customer."

The woman's face bloomed into a glowing expression of delight. "I am?"

Brody said, "She is?"

Max nudged Brody in the ribs to get him to hush.

Gwen stifled a giggle.

"She is." Drew waved away her money. "Merry Christmas from Teaberry Farms."

With a chuckle, Max wrapped his gloved hand around the trunk of the tree and angled his head to Brody, indicating that Brody should follow him. They loaded the woman's tree onto the roof of her beaten-up car. As she drove off Brody looked from the woman's car to his dad and back again, shaking his head.

Drew was smoother with the next customer, an elderly gentleman with two grandkids dancing around his legs.

Drew glanced at the tree, then the man, then the kids, and said, "Ten dollars."

The man happily paid, and Max and Brody loaded the tree. This time Brody didn't appear to be confused. He actually smiled.

Realizing there wasn't a break in the line of customers for her to pull Drew away, Gwen walked to the counter and handed his fax to him.

"Thanks."

"You're welcome."

She should have turned away and gone back to the house, but all she could do was stare at him. He'd given away the tree so kindly, so naturally, that only she, Max and Brody had recognized his generosity. She suddenly understood why she was so drawn to him. Deep down he was a good man.

A very good man. Her instincts had known it all along. That was why she kept forgetting there were too many differences between them for them to have a relationship. That was why she'd gotten so depressed when he'd reminded her the night before that they should keep their distance. She *wanted* a relationship with him.

Drew nodded toward the house. "You should go back in. It's cold."

She might want a relationship with him, but he didn't want one with her. She had to accept that.

Without looking at him she said, "Okay," and walked to the house. But at the front door she paused and glanced back at him, just in time to see him fold the fax and put it in his pocket so he could serve the next customer. He was putting his tree customers before his conglomerate.

She opened the front door and stepped inside the house. If he were hers, she'd tell him what a wonderful guy he was. But he wasn't hers. He would never be hers.

The tree farm didn't officially close for the day until after eight. Gwen took sandwiches and coffee out to the men at one for lunch, and again at six, but she had a real dinner waiting for them when they came in for the night.

Drew didn't even look at her when he said, "Thanks."

She smiled anyway. "You're welcome."

Brody snorted and kicked off his boots. "*Thanks. You're welcome.* You can stop the act. I get it."

Drew cast a horrified glance in his son's direction. "What are you talking about?"

"You're trying to teach me better manners. I get it. But you can stop now."

Obviously tired from the day's work, Drew looked like a

man who had reached his limit. Gwen wasn't surprised when he exploded.

"Why are you so grouchy?"

Brody rounded on him. "Me? Grouchy? You bring me to the pit from hell, put me to work, then constantly act super-polite around me with Gwen, as if you're walking on eggshells."

Gwen's breath caught in her throat. He thought they were walking on eggshells because of *him?* She saw a corresponding look of horror come to Drew's face.

Luckily, he recovered quickly. "I'm sorry, but Gwen and I aren't walking on eggshells because of you. We're professionals. A boss and his assistant, trying to get our work done."

"Then why do I hear you talking nicer to each other when I'm not around and only being super-polite when I am?"

Gwen coughed uncomfortably.

Drew shook his head. "I don't know what to say, Brody—"

Neither did Gwen. Was it appropriate to tell Drew's sixteen-year-old son that they were fighting their attraction and that was why they were so stiff and polite with each other?

Brody blew his breath out. "Right. You don't know what to say. You never know what to say because I'm a pain in your butt. An extra person underfoot that you don't need right now. Why don't you just ship me off, like mom did?"

"Hey, look, Brody, this might not be convenient for you, but your mom is on her honeymoon. Give her a break."

Brody snorted. "You still think she's taking me back, don't you? I'll bet you never even called her to ask if what I'd told you was true." He shook his head. "You know, Dad, for a smart guy you can make it amazingly easy for someone to pull the wool over your eyes."

As he said that, Brody shoved his boots to the corner by the door and stormed out of the room.

In the silence that followed, Drew's gaze strayed over to

Gwen. She smiled sympathetically, but embarrassment rose up in her. It was hard being attracted to someone and not being able to show it. They'd flubbed this deal royally.

Drew shook his head. "I don't even know where to start with the apologies."

"You don't need to apologize to me. But I do think you need to call Brody's mom. That's the second time he's said she doesn't want him back. The first time I thought he was just exaggerating to make himself look put upon, but now I'm not so sure."

Drew sighed. "Yeah. I'm going to have to call." He glanced at the table. "Sorry about ruining dinner."

She waved a hand in dismissal. "Everything will keep until you and Brody get this straightened out."

"And if we don't?"

"You'll eat it as leftovers tomorrow."

Drew couldn't help it; he burst out laughing. Was it any wonder he found Gwen irresistible? In the face of all the trouble they'd had with Brody, she managed to not only give him good advice but also to make him laugh.

But when he dropped to the seat behind the desk and dialed the number for Olivia's cell phone, he forgot all about Gwen and braced himself for a difficult conversation—if only because his conversations with Olivia were always difficult. He didn't beat around the bush or waste time. He simply came right out and asked if she planned on taking Brody back after her honeymoon. She didn't mince words, either. Now that she had a new husband she wanted a new life. Brody was officially Drew's responsibility.

He spent ten minutes alone in the office after he disconnected the call. He didn't know whether to be angry because Olivia had handled this so poorly or scared to death because he now had the care of a sixteen-year-old who clearly didn't like him.

Gwen was still at the table when he returned to the kitchen.

She faced him eagerly. "Well?"

He took a seat across from her and blew his breath out on a heavy sigh. "She wants me to keep him."

Her face scrunched warily. "Is that good or bad?"

"Well, I work a lot—"

"You can fit Brody in. In the two weeks you've been here you've managed to find eight hours a day to run a Christmas tree farm, keep your conglomerate going, and continue to negotiate to buy a new business."

"Only because I pawned a lot of work off on my vice-presidents."

She laughed merrily. "So? Keep doing that."

Catching her gaze, he relaxed on his chair. "I guess I could."

"You hired those people for a reason. I'll bet they're thrilled to be getting more responsibility." She put her elbow on the table and her chin on her fist and smiled at him. "What else?"

He winced. "Now I have to tell Brody that he was right. He will be living with me." He blew his breath out. "I have no idea what to say."

Gwen glanced down at the table, thinking of her own dad, wondering how she would have felt if he'd suddenly gotten custody of her and Gill. Her mom would have had to have been deathly ill to give them up, and Gwen would have been terrified to live with the dad who hadn't wanted her.

Drew snorted a laugh. "How can I expect to be a good father when I don't even know how to tell him he's now living with me?"

She slowly raised her gaze to meet Drew's. "My dad left my mom when Gill and I were born."

Drew frowned, obviously not understanding why she'd said that.

She plugged on, talking about the most humiliating, most difficult situation in her life. "Mom said he was expecting one baby and got two." She shrugged. "It freaked him out. And—" She sucked in a breath. "If he had suddenly gotten custody of us, I would have been terrified."

"I suppose so. You didn't know him?"

She shook her head. "No. That isn't what would have frightened me. I would have been terrified because I knew he didn't want us. I don't know the guy, so I couldn't have said he would have beaten us or not fed us or anything like that. But can you imagine living with someone who ignored you? Or complained about having you around?"

Drew's eyes narrowed. "Are you saying Brody's acting out because he's afraid I don't want him?"

"I don't know. But think it through. How would you feel if the mother you loved suddenly didn't want you anymore and the dad you were sent to live with didn't really have time for you?"

Drew squeezed his eyes shut. Several seconds passed in absolute silence. Then he rose from his seat and headed out of the kitchen.

Thinking she'd screwed up with her advice, since Drew wasn't really anything like her totally absent father, Gwen scrambled after him. But he was quicker than she was. By the time she got to Brody's room he was already inside.

"I want you."

Gwen skidded to a stop in front of the open door, just in time to see Brody glare up at his dad from his position on the bed. "Big whoop."

Drew sat on the bed beside Brody's long legs. "It is a big whoop. I missed your baby years. I missed elementary school. I missed middle school. But not by choice. Your mom moved you far away." He looked down, then back up at Brody again. "It's a blessing for me to get you. I may only have two years before you're off to university, but I want those years. I want every minute I can get with you to get to know you."

Brody's eyes narrowed. "Really?"

"Yes. I think the next two years with you might be the happiest of my life."

Brody unexpectedly bounced up and grabbed his father in a hug. Tears filled Gwen's eyes and she backed out of the room, leaving father and son to their personal moment.

But when Drew returned to the kitchen she didn't hesitate. She said, "That was the sweetest thing I've ever seen anybody do," caught the front of his shirt, pulled him to her, and kissed him.

CHAPTER SEVEN

She tasted his passion first. Surprised as he had been, he reacted instinctively and naturally fell into the kiss. All his pent-up desires rushed out in one fierce press of his mouth to hers. But as quickly as that registered for Gwen he shifted, changed. As if suddenly realizing he was finally getting what he'd been itching to take, he tempered his passion, and he smoothed his lips over hers gently, experimentally.

She rose to her tiptoes and kissed him back. She glided her hands up his arms to his shoulders. His arms slid around her waist as his tongue slipped into her mouth.

Sweet fire exploded in her veins, rocking her to her core. It took several seconds for the world to right itself, but when it did he twined his tongue with hers and the fire inside her roared with life and energy. No simple kiss had ever affected her as this one did, and when his hands slid up her back, tightening her more snugly against him, she suspected the kiss was as explosive for him as it was for her.

She knew why. They truly liked each other. All along they'd had sexual chemistry, but adding emotion to that chemistry had made them a fiery combination. She couldn't even begin to imagine what it would be like to actually make love to him if a kiss could reduce her to a simmering bundle of need.

But before she could take her thoughts any further he

released her, stepped back and rubbed his hands down his face. "I'm sorry."

"Don't be sorry! That was great. Plus, I started it. What you did with Brody was fantastic. No woman could resist that."

Self-conscious, he took another step back. "It was still wrong. And we can't do that again. You're so young, Gwen. You have your whole life ahead of you. I'm settled with who I am and what I have, and now I have a sixteen-year-old son to raise. Hell, you're barely older than he is. I won't get involved with you."

With that he strode out of the kitchen, and Gwen fell despondently to one of the chairs around the table. She wasn't sorry she'd kissed him. But she was sorry about the age gap between them. How could she possibly fight that? Change that? She couldn't.

With the awkward way Drew treated her over the next few days Gwen was glad she hadn't started the practice of spending the night—though she had packed pajamas for herself and Claire, just in case the weather was truly too bad for her to drive in.

Drew was careful to be cheerful around Brody, so there was no doubt that he was wanted, but around her he was withdrawn, as if he were afraid that one kind word would cause her to kiss him again. She should have been embarrassed, but she wasn't. How could she be embarrassed about kissing a man she genuinely liked? Someone she knew liked her, too?

On Tuesday afternoon Drew brought in the Christmas tree he'd promised her, and set it up in the living room without a word. She'd found an old tree stand and he shoved it inside, but couldn't secure it. Not waiting to be asked, she rushed to help him. When they both reached for the same spot on the tree trunk their hands brushed.

Awareness twinkled from her hand to her heart. Her feelings for him were so strong that her chest swelled with longing. He caught her gaze, glanced at their hands, then slowly moved his fingers higher on the trunk.

This time her chest squeezed with pain. He clearly hadn't changed his mind. She wanted a relationship. She had kissed him. He'd kissed her back, only to rebuff her. He didn't want her.

Maybe she should just accept that?

After that, she continued to cook for the Teaberrys, but she stopped eating with them and forgot all about staying overnight.

But on Friday night, when Max and Brody came into the house after their day's work, Max laughed at the fact that she was in her coat, ready to run out and start her car before she and Claire left for home.

"You might as well sit down and have some of that chicken you made for us," he said, shrugging out of his coat.

Avoiding even accidentally meeting Drew's gaze by looking at the floor, she said, "I can't stay tonight."

"You're going to have to." Brody laughed and pulled out a chair. "Last customer said the mountain road is blowing shut."

She lifted her head and gaped at Brody. "Blowing shut?"

Max chuckled as he also took a seat at the table. "That wind is fierce! Have you been so busy you haven't even heard the storm?"

Not busy. Preoccupied with making sure Drew didn't see how hurt she was by his not wanting her. She glanced down at her baby, happily cooing in the carrier, already dressed in her snowsuit.

Drew walked to the stove. "You take care of Claire. Get her settled for the night. I'll get the food on the table."

Appalled that she'd been so nervous all day she hadn't even noticed the storm moving in, she raced back to her bedroom, tossed Claire's diaper bag to the bed, shrugged out of her coat and undressed her baby, chastising herself for being an idiot.

Still, when she went back into the kitchen she pretended her staying the night was no big deal, asking Max and Brody about their days, enjoying their company. After dinner she persuaded Brody to help with the dishes, and he happily complied.

When Drew tried to join them she took the stack of cups from his hands. "Why don't you go back to the office and finish reading the most recent e-mail from Jimmy Lane?"

"Because it's Friday night and I'd already decided we weren't going to work."

She shook her head. "It's a big deal that he finally got back to you with a serious e-mail countering your last offer. You can't ignore it. Go. We'll be fine."

Then she turned away, faced the sink, and wouldn't even look back until she was absolutely positive he'd left the room.

After finishing reading the e-mail Gwen had all but demanded he read, Drew walked to the living room, where Max had laid a fire in the marble fireplace. Instead of finding the room empty, as he'd expected, he found Brody and Gwen decorating the Christmas tree. Little Claire sat in her carrier on the sofa.

"Hey, Dad!" Brody said, pointing at a box of ornaments. "Dig in. This tree is huge. We can use all the help we can get."

"That's okay, I'll—"

"Stay," Gwen said, her gaze drifting over to his before she

nudged her head in Brody's direction, as if telling him his staying would be good for Brody.

He hesitated. She looked cute in a pair of Santa-covered flannel pajamas that matched the one-piece pajamas worn by Claire, whose eyes were glued to the lights twinkling on the tree. Brody had showered, and wore red and green plaid pajama pants and a red T-shirt. With the tree behind them, they could have been the picture on a Christmas card.

He stepped into the room. "I don't know how much help I'll be."

Gwen handed Brody an ornament to hang at the top of the tree. "Haven't you ever done this before?" she asked jokingly.

But he replied seriously. "I go to my parents for Christmas dinner and spend twelve-hour days at the office. Not much point in having a tree in my condo."

"Then it's lucky you're learning how to decorate one," Brody said, teasing the way Gwen was. "Because I'll want a tree."

"And you'll want a tree now, too, Drew," Gwen said, handing Brody a colored ball to hang near the gold star at the top of the tree. She caught Drew's gaze, sending him another signal by glancing at Brody, then back at him. "Didn't you tell me that you were going to start delegating more of your work to your vice-presidents, so you could have more time at home?"

"Yes," Drew answered quickly, glad she'd brought that up because he hadn't really told Brody that part of the plan.

Not wanting his nervousness to show when he spoke, he grabbed an ornament and walked around the back of the tree, to the side in front of the window, away from both Gwen and Brody, and began decorating there.

"While I've been here, I've only really worked half-days."

He peered around the tree at Brody. "Not that I'm going to cut my schedule in half now that you're living with me, but I *can* see that it would be possible to only work eight-hour days if I delegate."

Brody said, "All right!"

Drew sighed with relief. "I was also thinking we should get a house."

Gwen peered over at him. "A house?"

"Yeah." He avoided her gaze. He'd thought about moving out of the condo and into a real house because of her. She'd made this shabby old house into a home—something he didn't think his streamlined condo could ever be. And a family needed a house. He and Brody might not be a big family, but they were still a family.

Brody danced for joy. "A beach house?"

Drew cautiously said, "Would you want to live on the beach?"

"Hell, yeah!"

Both Drew and Gwen said, "Don't say hell."

Brody laughed. "This is great!" He pulled his cell phone from a pocket in his pajama pants. "I have to text my friends."

With that he zipped out of the room, and Drew froze. Except for when they worked together at night, this was the first time he'd been alone with Gwen since their kiss, and he absolutely didn't know what to say. He knew he'd hurt her. He'd hurt himself. Brushing her off after that kiss had been the hardest thing he'd ever done. He'd thought about it for days afterward. Mourned the decision he knew he had to make.

"A house sounds like a good idea."

"Yeah." He picked up another ornament for the tree and looped around to the back side, avoiding her. "A condo's no place for a kid. He'll need room to roam."

"On the ocean? Is he going to walk on water?"

Her comment made him laugh. Again. She always knew how to make him laugh. "No, he'll have miles of beach to walk on." He sucked in a breath. "I'm probably going to have to get him an ATV. A surfboard. A boogey board. Scuba gear."

"You're going to be busy."

He laughed. "It feels weird."

"But I'll bet it's a good weird."

It was. "Had you told me two weeks ago that I'd be looking forward to living with Brody I would have thought you were nuts."

She chuckled. "Haven't you *ever* thought about having Brody with you for longer than two weeks?"

Using the tree for protection, he answered honestly. "Yes. Because I was an only child I'd grown up thinking how much fun it would be to have a big family." He shrugged. "But a few years after Brody was born I settled to just have him with me for one holiday."

"Why didn't you try for more?"

"Because I knew Olivia would fight me. I didn't want Brody to see us fighting or risk losing the scant visitation I had."

"Sad."

"Yeah."

She walked around to his side of the tree. "So why didn't you find another wife? Have more kids?"

He busied himself hanging a candy cane and didn't answer.

After a minute or two of silence, Gwen said, "You're a natural Christmas tree decorator."

He laughed. "It's not exactly rocket science."

"I have some cocoa and cookies on the table if you want some."

Grateful that she hadn't pursued her question about another

wife and kids, he walked around the other side of the tree, so he didn't accidentally brush against her. He didn't know how to answer her. What could he say? He'd been too busy? He had been, but tonight that reason seemed lame.

When he reached down to get a gingerbread man he found himself at eye-level with Claire.

She cooed at him.

His heart melted. It was the first time he'd been this close to her, so he'd never before noticed that her eyes were dark—not green, like her mom's, but almost black, like Drew's. Her hair was the same color as her mom's, though. Shiny, silky blond.

She cooed again.

He set the cookie back on the plate and inched over to her. He gingerly extended his index finger and ran it along the velvety skin of her hand. He couldn't stop his whispered, "Wow."

"I know," Gwen said from behind him. "She's adorable."

"And soft." He cautiously turned his head and caught Gwen's gaze. "I'd forgotten how soft babies are."

"It sounds like Brody's first months of life weren't easy for you—not something you wanted to remember."

He sucked in a breath. "No." And maybe that was why he'd never found another wife? The one he'd had had soured him on marriage. "Those years aren't something I like to remember."

She snagged a gingerbread man and eased over to the tree again. Picking up a striped ball, she said, "Have you ever stopped to think that maybe you're not opposed to us trying a relationship because of my age as much as because you're afraid?"

He spun around. "What?"

"Your first marriage sounds like it was pretty bad. I don't

know your ex-wife, and I could be way off base, but from the way she handled giving you custody of Brody she seems like she might have been—" She sucked in a breath. "Self-centered."

He laughed at her choice of words. "She was worse than self-centered."

She waited until he looked over at her before she said, "Not all women are like her."

The truth of that shimmied through him, because Gwen was the living, breathing evidence of what she'd said. But it didn't change the fact that she was twelve years younger than he was.

"I get what you're saying. And I agree. My first marriage *was* abysmal. But this thing between us is wrong." He glanced at Claire, then back at Gwen. "How about if we just go back to decorating the tree and forget all about my first marriage?"

She smiled. "Okay."

He couldn't believe how easily she'd agreed, but then guessed the conversation had probably been difficult for her, too. They continued decorating the tree in silence. Gwen's baby cooed as Gwen's hands busily adjusted the ornaments so they were just perfect. Brody returned to the room and began happily chatting about his friends' reactions to Brody living at the beach.

And Drew's heart broke. For the first time in his life he was experiencing a glimpse of the life he'd always wanted. And it was with a woman he couldn't have.

CHAPTER EIGHT

THE next day was December twenty-second. Three days till Christmas. Customers formed a non-stop line on the tree-lined lane to Teaberry Farms, and Gwen bundled up twice that day to bring hot cocoa to grateful Drew, Max and Brody.

But on her second trip she looked up from handing Drew a cup of cocoa and saw the woman who had "won" the free tree. This time she wasn't wearing the tattered blue coat. She wore a black leather jacket, black boots, and carried a purse Gwen knew cost over a thousand dollars.

Her mouth fell open. After waiting for Drew to finish with his customer, she caught his arm and dragged him a few feet away from the stand. "Remember the woman you said was the one-hundredth customer so you could give her a tree?"

He nodded. "Yes."

"She's back. In line."

Drew peered at the trail of customers. "No, she's not."

"Yes, she is. She's wearing an expensive black coat and boots, and carrying a bag that costs more than I'll make in a month when I start teaching."

Drew glanced out at the line again. When he saw the woman Gwen referred to his eyes narrowed. "That *is* her." He swung his gaze back to Gwen. "I gave a rich woman a free tree."

Brody sidled over to them. "Maybe she just got a Christmas tree wish?"

Max growled, "Stop making fun of the legend," before he picked up the tree Drew had just sold and headed off with Brody to secure it on top of the car of the customer.

Drew said, "So what do we do?"

"Nothing. Unless you want to charge her double for the tree she's about to buy?"

Drew shook his head. "Nope. I was duped. My loss."

Gwen nodded, but stood at the cash box with him and helped him collect the money for the trees as the well-dressed woman approached. When it was her turn, Gwen stopped what she was doing and watched Drew.

Instead of being angry, or even annoyed, he pretended not to know her. "Merry Christmas," he said, the same way he had to the ten customers he'd handled before her. "That'll be thirty dollars."

She happily opened her wallet and handed him the money, but before he could take it she sighed. "Okay. I saw you guys pointing at me, and I'm guessing you remember me from the other day."

Drew crossed his arms on his chest. "We do. We gave you a free tree."

"And really impressed me." She extended her hand across the cash counter. "I'm Jimmy Lane."

Gwen's mouth fell open. All this time Drew had thought he was negotiating with a cranky old man, and instead "Jimmy" was a gorgeous young woman in a sexy leather coat and boots, with blond hair that fell past her shoulders and bright blue eyes.

When neither Drew nor Gwen spoke, she laughed. "I get it," she said, glancing from shell-shocked Drew to Gwen, then back to Drew again. "You thought you were dealing with my grandfather."

Drew was the first to find his voice. "Yes."

"Well, you were," Jimmy said. "I'm his namesake and his replacement. I was the one typing the e-mails, but he had the final say on everything that went into them. He sent me here to check up on you. You passed with flying colors when you gave the woman you thought was poor a free tree. My grandfather is now convinced you're the perfect person to own his company." She jostled her tree in Drew's direction. "By the way, I still want to buy this tree."

"You already have one," Gwen said sourly, then nearly bit her tongue, hardly believing she'd been so rude. She wasn't angry that the woman had finagled a tree. Jimmy had had her reasons for her ruse, and she hadn't asked Drew to give her a tree. So Gwen had no idea why she couldn't be nice to her.

"We have a big house. We put up six trees. My grandfather can't get enough of Christmas."

"Sounds like my grandfather," Drew said as he headed for the cash register. Gwen almost thought he'd give the tree to Jimmy as another gesture of good will, until she suddenly realized that this was a business transaction. Jimmy and Drew were business people. Equals. The Lanes weren't about to give him a discount on the company he was buying from them. He wasn't about to give them a discount on the tree they were buying from him. And Jimmy didn't expect one. She easily opened her wallet and pulled out the cash.

It was like she and Drew were on the same page.

Gwen's eyes narrowed. They *were* on the same page. About the same age. Raised in luxury. Groomed to take over the family holdings. Smart, educated, attractive.

She glanced down at her worn parka and boots. How the devil had she ever thought Drew might want *her*?

As Drew made change, Jimmy glanced around. "You know, I'm sort of sorry I won't be coming back. This place is gorgeous."

"Thanks."

"So where is your real home?"

"North Carolina."

"My family has a beach house in Charleston." She smiled. "Maybe we could get together some time?"

Drew inclined his head. "Why? Does your conglomerate have other companies you're looking to sell?"

Jimmy smiled at Max as he hoisted the tree to take it to her SUV. "Thanks."

But the smile she gave to Drew when she faced him again had nothing to do with business. "Yes, we do have other companies we could sell, but I also make a wicked lasagna and have a wine collection that will knock your socks off."

Gwen's breath shivered in her chest. Jimmy had blatantly flirted with Drew in front of Gwen. Why? Because Gwen was an employee. A servant. Jimmy had dismissed her as being unimportant.

Gwen had to fight the anger that welled up inside of her. Mostly because she didn't know who she was angry with. Jimmy for dismissing her? Drew for being the perfect match for Jimmy? Or herself for being an idiot, thinking she was made for somebody like Drew?

She turned in the snow and headed back into the house. The sound of Claire crying or even awakening hadn't come through the baby monitor, but right now Gwen needed to see her baby to feel loved, wanted. She slipped off her boots by the kitchen door and headed for the maid's quarters.

She shook her head. She was even staying in the maid's quarters. Like the servant she was. Yet she'd fallen in love with a man who didn't want her. Hell, he'd even told her that.

Seeing that Claire was still sound asleep, she headed out of the room to make dinner just as Drew stepped inside. Before Gwen could slip out of his way he caught her around the waist and danced her around the room.

"She approved our last version of the agreement."

Gwen pulled herself out of his arms. "Well, she did say her grandfather had already called you the perfect person to buy his company."

"I know! Isn't it fantastic? Honestly, I think I got one of Max's Christmas tree miracles."

Avoiding his gaze, she puttered around her bedroom, feeling odd that he felt at ease being in her sleeping quarters until she realized that to him this wasn't a bedroom. It was the maid's quarters.

"Don't you feel like celebrating?"

She tried to smile, but couldn't. Fact upon fact bombarded her. What right did she have to celebrate Drew's purchase of a business? In just a few minutes in Jimmy's company Gwen had easily seen Jimmy was the kind of woman Drew belonged with. Even if he got carried away in the enthusiasm of the moment, told Gwen he loved her, asked her to marry him, they didn't belong together. He'd been right all along.

Tears stung her eyes. Stupidly, she'd fallen in love with a man who wouldn't ever love her.

She swallowed and turned away. "You know what? I just realized that with the agreement for the purchase finalized my work is done."

"Yeah. So now we celebrate." He tried to catch her, probably to turn her to face him, but she skittered away.

"It's three days till Christmas, Drew. I've been almost living here for weeks now. My house isn't cleaned for the holiday, or decorated."

He stepped back. "What?"

She pressed her hand to her chest. "I need to go home."

"Oh."

"It's Claire's first Christmas. She loves your tree, but I'd like to give her one of my own."

Watching Gwen's little red car disappear down the country road, Drew swallowed the lump in his throat. This was for the best. They weren't right for each other. No matter how much it hurt to see her drive away, he had to let her go.

With another six hours of selling trees to get through, he took his position at the cash register and lost himself in the crush of Christmas tree customers. Once word had circulated that the farm was open, people had come from miles around to get their trees. Most older customers had a story about a miracle that had happened in their lives after buying one of their trees. Drew shook his head sadly. He'd thought getting Jimmy Lane's company was his miracle, but now that Gwen was gone he had to admit the purchase of one more company for an already burgeoning conglomerate felt empty. Hollow.

The second they closed that night, as Max waved goodbye to go home, and Brody happily turned off the lights strung across the outbuildings and lit the cheery colored bulbs lighting the fir trees around the mansion, Drew's heart sank. It was the first night since they'd been here that Gwen wouldn't be there. There'd be no dinner. No gingerbread. No muffins. No warmth. No joy.

He followed Brody into the house, not saying a word when his son announced he was running upstairs for his shower.

Twenty minutes later, when Brody returned to the kitchen, his flushed cheeks made his bright blue eyes seem even brighter. Drew hadn't ever seen his son this youthfully excited over a holiday. Though he'd like to take the credit, he couldn't. Gwen had decorated the house. Gwen had made the place smell like heaven. Gwen had even given him the advice he'd needed to make Brody happy.

"Where is everybody?"

Drew pulled in a breath. "Gwen has gone home."

It hurt to even say the words, so he turned back to the stove, his grim mood becoming downright sour.

"What do you mean, she's gone home? They're staying here."

The grilled cheese sandwiches Drew was cooking to go with the canned vegetable soup heating on the pot beside the grill weren't very appetizing, especially compared to the wonderful meals Gwen had prepared for them, but they were warm and filling, and after all the work he'd done that day, Brody should be hungry enough to be grateful for it—not taking Drew to task for something that was none of his business.

"Son, the deal is done now, and Gwen needed to get herself ready for Christmas. I'm sure her sister will get time off for the holiday, and Gwen wants to spend time with her twin—her family."

Brody unexpectedly caught his dad's upper arm and spun him away from the stove. His eyes sparked with anger. His breaths came in short puffs. "She *was* with family. Us!"

Surprised by the strength Brody had acquired working only a few short weeks, Drew nonetheless didn't back down. "No. She wasn't. We're not her family."

Brody held his ground, too. "Yes, we are."

Suddenly tired, Drew faced the stove, snapped off the now bubbling soup and flipped the cheese sandwiches. "Brody, we came here for a month. I'd like to come back every Christmas, to open the tree farm, but Gwen McKenzie is a young woman who is just starting her life—"

"Is that what this is all about?" Brody asked, his voice

dripping with so much surprise that Drew peered over his shoulder.

"What?"

"You're afraid."

"I'm not afraid," Drew blustered, annoyed because Gwen had suggested the same thing.

"Sure you are. You like Gwen, but you're afraid of getting married."

Drew's jaw dropped. "Brody, this is none of your business!"

"It is! Dad, just because your marriage to Mom didn't work out that doesn't mean you should stop trying!"

"I didn't stop trying."

"Really? Then why do you hardly even date?"

"I date."

"Okay, then why haven't you married any of those women?"

"Because we didn't click."

"You clicked with Gwen. I saw it. Yet I'll bet you never even kissed her."

Drew's face heated. He couldn't believe he was having this conversation, and prayed he could figure out a way to get out of it.

"You *did* kiss her! You *do* like her! You do click with her but you're afraid."

"Brody, I'm so much older than she is!"

"That's an excuse. Come on, Dad. If you're going to let her leave, at least be honest with yourself about why."

With that Brody grabbed a sandwich and left the kitchen. Drew sat at the table and ran his hand down his face. One month ago he'd been a lonely single guy who could do what he wanted. Now he had custody of a sixteen-year-old who didn't hesitate to interfere in his life and his broken heart.

He stopped.

He did have a broken heart. A seriously broken heart. And Gwen did, too. One word from him—or maybe three words from him—could fix both their hearts, yet he couldn't say them.

He ran his hand down his face again. Was Brody right? Was Gwen right? Was he simply afraid?

CHAPTER NINE

GWEN got off the phone with Gill the next morning and wiped tears from her eyes. It was now official. Her life sucked. Not only had Andrew Teaberry let her go, as if she were any other employee, but now Gill couldn't come home for Christmas. She had time off, but had waited too long to make airline reservations and now couldn't get a flight home.

Gwen's baby's first Christmas would be a small, lonely event spent with only her mom.

But at least she'd have gifts and a tree and any kind of food she wanted—not that she could eat food—because Drew had wired her salary into her account and he'd added five thousand dollars more than what she'd negotiated when she'd agreed to help him clean the house.

Part of her wanted to call him and tell him she wouldn't take his charity. The other part absolutely refused to have any more contact with him. She loved him. He'd broken her heart. She'd keep the damn five thousand dollars before she'd risk seeing him again.

With Claire down for her morning nap, Gwen's house was eerily quiet. Even when she and Claire had been alone in Drew's house the hum of the wind through the mountain pass had kept her company. The knowledge that there were other people living in that house had made her feel secure, bonded, almost as if she were in a family.

But that was her problem. She'd grown accustomed to things that weren't hers and now she had to face the truth. Drew hadn't wanted her. She wasn't part of his family. She was alone.

She turned to go into her kitchen, but before she took two steps there was a quick rap at her door. Expecting it to be a delivery man with her gift from Gill, she pivoted and raced to the door. With one quick yank she opened it, and there stood Drew, holding a tree.

Her heart wanted her to believe he'd come because he'd realized that he was wrong. That their age difference didn't matter. That he was a young thirty-four and she was a mature twenty-two. That he could love her. That he *did* love her.

But her head remembered that he'd let her leave. That he'd given her extra money to salve his conscience. That he didn't want her.

"Hello, Drew."

With his fingers wrapped around the trunk of a blue spruce, Drew simply stared at her. Finally he cleared his throat and said, "I, um, thought it weird that you'd worked at a Christmas tree farm for an entire month and we never thought to get you a tree for your house."

Her heart sank again. He was only here to give her a tree. Worse, seeing him brought nothing but craziness and confusion for her. When she should be keeping her distance, caring for her own broken heart, all she could think of was that he looked tired, drawn, and fearful—as if he expected her to slam the door in his face.

Well, she wouldn't. He was right. She didn't have a tree. And getting one from Teaberry Farms seemed appropriate.

"Thank you." She averted her eyes and motioned for him to come in. "Bring it inside."

Drew stepped into her foyer. "Where do you want it?"

"The corner by the stairway is where my mom always had it," Gwen said, then choked up as she remembered the happy Christmas Eves she and her sister had spent decorating the tree with their mom. This might be their second holiday without her, but the memories and pain were still fresh, like an open wound.

Gwen turned away. She missed her mom. She missed being a little girl who had enjoyed every magical Christmas. Though she loved Claire with her whole heart and soul, she'd screwed up by trusting a man who didn't really love her. And now she'd fallen in love—real love—with another man who didn't want her.

The living room suddenly became quiet. Gwen refused to turn around. With tears shimmering on her eyelids, she headed for the kitchen. "I'll make cocoa while you put the tree into the stand."

Not in any hurry, Gwen found the milk, powdered cocoa, sugar and vanilla, and slowly began her brew. By the time she returned to the living room Drew had installed the tree into the old tree stand.

As she entered the room he took the tray from her hands and set it on the coffee table. "Can we talk?"

"I think you've said everything that needs to be said."

He looked away, then back at her. "Sometimes I can be an ass."

His unexpected comment made her laugh. That was one of the things she loved about him. He had a serious job, a great deal of responsibilities, yet he had a sense of humor. Or maybe she'd helped him find his sense of humor?

"Okay."

A hopeful expression came to his face. "I'm sorry I let you go." He stopped. Sighed. "Actually, Brody was genuinely annoyed with me for that. But the point is I shouldn't have."

Gwen stared at him. *Was he offering her a job?* Damned if she knew. But there was no way in hell she was going to say anything and risk misinterpreting him. No way she'd embarrass herself. So she stayed silent, hoping against hope he was not trying to hire her back.

Especially since most of the work she'd done for him had been house-cleaning and he might want her back as his maid!

He rubbed his hand across the back of his neck. "I am so bad at this because I've never said anything like it. I screwed up by telling you our age difference should keep us apart."

Gwen's heart leaped with hope, but she still stayed silent. Unless or until he told her he loved her, she wasn't making any assumptions.

Struggling, Drew glanced around the room. His gaze landed on the tree.

"Okay, tree, I'm not much on magic or miracles or things like that, but right now I need some help." He drew a breath. "I wish Gwen would give me another chance. I screwed everything up by being afraid. I know I was wrong. That's why I need another chance."

Gwen blinked tears from her eyes. She knew how hard this was for him. Knew that he was putting himself out on a limb, trusting her, when the last time he'd trusted a woman he'd not only gotten his heart broken but that woman had taken his son away from him.

Now the ball was in her court. If she didn't trust him she'd hurt him more than he'd ever hurt her.

"You don't need magic to get a second chance," she whispered, praying she was making the right choice. "You only have to tell me you love me."

"I love you."

He held out his arms and she raced into them.

He kissed her hair. "Your life's not going to be easy with me."

She put her arms around his neck. Warmth suffused her. So did joy. "Do you think I haven't already figured that out?"

He slid his arms around her waist. "Oh, yeah? What have you figured out?"

"That you're accustomed to perfection. That you're intense about your family's business. That you want everything done right and well."

"I'll make room for you. I swear."

"Have you ever stopped to think you won't have to make room for me? That I'll fit? And maybe even having me around might ease your burden a bit?"

He smiled slowly. "Someone to come home to at night," he said as his head began to descend.

"Someone to have dinner waiting."

"Or be waiting at the door wearing nothing but a smile."

With that his lips met hers, and her giggle was swallowed up by his mouth.

Christmas morning, and Gwen was in the kitchen of the Teaberry mansion. She'd found all the ingredients for apple cinnamon muffins, and as her baby chewed on a rattle she set about to make the kitchen smell warm and sweet.

She was just pulling the last tin of muffins from the oven when Drew walked into the kitchen.

She smiled at him. "Hey."

He ambled over sleepily. "Hey. What are you doing up so early?"

"It's eight. Besides, Claire's been up since six-thirty. She didn't wake in the middle of the night, so I guess getting up early was her way to make up for that."

He stopped her words with a kiss.

When he pulled away, she smiled at him. "Merry Christmas."

"Merry Christmas." He laughed. "I have to say you're probably the best Christmas present I've ever gotten."

"I hope so, because I didn't have time to buy you anything."

"Which reminds me—" He turned toward the swinging door. "Wanna come in now?"

The kitchen door swung open slowly, and there stood Gill.

Gwen screamed with joy. Gill screamed with delight. They ran into each other's arms.

Drew said, "Claire didn't really sleep through the night. She woke when Gill got here." He laughed as the twins hugged each other. "But I got her a bottle."

Gwen pulled out of Gill's hug. "I don't know what shocks me more. That you somehow got Gill here—"

"Private plane," Drew supplied.

"Or that you took care of Claire."

"Hey, I've got to start sometime."

Gill laughed, walked to the counter and glanced at the muffins. "Are these apple cinnamon?"

Gwen nodded, "Yes."

"All right!" She headed for the refrigerator. "I'll make bacon."

Brody stepped into the room. He glanced at Gwen, then Gill, and laughed. "You must be the twin."

"Gill," Gwen supplied.

Gill said, "You must be Brody."

Brody nodded. "So, what are we making?"

"Apple cinnamon muffins and bacon," Gill said. "Then we open presents."

Brody's face brightened. "You got *me* something?"

Gill winced. "At the gift shop in the airport."

Brody laughed. "I am going to love having an aunt."

Drew leaned against the countertop, admiring his wife-to-be, loving his new *family*.

Brody was right. He had been afraid. Or maybe he'd simply been waiting for the right woman? Either way, he'd like to live on Teaberry Farms for the rest of his life—where wishes came true and families were formed.

But it wouldn't matter where he lived so long as Gwen was with him.

* * * * *

Get 2 Books FREE!

Harlequin® Books,
publisher of women's fiction,
presents

GET 2 BOOKS

We'd like to send you two *Harlequin® Romance* novels absolutely free.
Accepting them puts you under no obligation to purchase any more books.

HOW TO GET YOUR
2 FREE BOOKS AND 2 FREE GIFTS

1. Return the reply card today, and we'll send you two *Harlequin Romance* novels, absolutely free! We'll even pay the postage!

2. Accepting free books places you under no obligation to buy anything, ever. Whatever you decide, the free books and gifts are yours to keep, free!

3. We hope that after receiving your free books you'll want to remain a subscriber, but the choice is yours—to continue or cancel, any time at all!

EXTRA BONUS

You'll also get two free mystery gifts! (worth about $10)

FREE!

Return this card promptly to get
2 FREE BOOKS and 2 FREE GIFTS!

YES! Please send me 2 FREE *Harlequin® Romance* novels, and 2 free mystery gifts as well. I understand I am under no obligation to purchase anything, as explained on the back of this insert.

About how many NEW paperback fiction books have you purchased in the past 3 months?

❏ 0-2	❏ 3-6	❏ 7 or more
E9J7	E9KK	E9KV

❏ I prefer the regular-print edition
116/316 HDL

❏ I prefer the larger-print edition
186/386 HDL

FIRST NAME	LAST NAME

ADDRESS

APT.#	CITY

STATE/PROV.	ZIP/POSTAL CODE

Visit us at:
www.ReaderService.com

▲ DETACH AND MAIL CARD TODAY! ▼

(H-R-11/10)

BUSINESS REPLY MAIL
FIRST-CLASS MAIL   PERMIT NO. 717   BUFFALO, NY

POSTAGE WILL BE PAID BY ADDRESSEE

THE READER SERVICE
PO BOX 1867
BUFFALO NY 14240-9952

NO POSTAGE
NECESSARY
IF MAILED
IN THE
UNITED STATES

BARBARA WALLACE

Magic Under the Mistletoe

Dear Reader,

Imagine how excited I was to learn I would be making my Harlequin Romance® debut with Susan Meier! Susan has long been one of my favorite authors, and working with her made my first writing assignment a joy. As we fleshed out the McKenzie twins' stories we discovered we had a lot in common, including a mutual appreciation for the magic surrounding Christmas—the kind that comes from opening your heart to the season's beauty and possibilities.

Workaholic Gill McKenzie is so bent on success she's forgotten what real Christmas magic is. Fortunately Oliver Harrington and his charges are there to remind her. And maybe, just maybe, open Oliver's eyes a little, too.

As for me, I'm enjoying the magic of being part of the Harlequin family. I hope you enjoy reading Gill's story as much as I enjoyed writing it. Meanwhile, on behalf of my husband and son here in New England, I wish you all a very Merry Christmas.

Happy holidays!

Barbara Wallace

Look out for Barbara Wallace's
next Harlequin Romance® novel in December
THE CINDERELLA BRIDE

CHAPTER ONE

THE brightly painted silhouettes of children decorating the McNabb Community Center couldn't mask its surroundings. Broken windows and padlocked storefronts told the truth. Across the street a group of young men, too young to be out of school, congregated in a convenience store doorway. Gill McKenzie felt them eyeing her as she stepped from the cab. An elderly woman pulling a metal shopping cart with groceries approached on the sidewalk. She too cast Gill a look as she passed.

Welcome to wrong side of the tracks.

Pulling out her cell phone, she double-checked the meeting time on her calendar and noted she had, as usual, arrived early. Punctuality was something she prided herself on. It showed clients you considered their projects important and of high priority.

Except this wasn't supposed to be her project, was it? She was *supposed* to handle the Remaillard aftershave launch. Remaillard was Rosenthal Public Relations' biggest client and organizing a successful product launch would have virtually guaranteed Gill the new vice-president position.

Enter Stephanie DeWitt. Gill could still hear the mock apology Stephanie gave during this morning's meeting. "I suggested to Elliot that you were the best person for the job.

What with your family owning a Christmas tree farm and all."

No, her brother-in-law owned the farm, Gill had wanted to scream. And Stephanie wanted the promotion as badly as she did. But Elliot Rosenthal had been right there, so she'd simply smiled graciously, seething inside.

So, while Stephanie took over the launch, with its big budget and luxury setting, Gill stood here, in the worst section of Boston, charged with throwing a kids' Christmas party. Not just any Christmas party. A magical, stunning, media-attention-generating party with less than a month's notice. Her only help was the center's director. Some guy named Oliver Harrington.

Across the street, the store owner chased the teenagers away, hollering what she was pretty sure were obscenities in Spanish. The kids swore back, and one of them tossed an empty can into the street. The rattle echoed in the frigid air. Gill sighed.

Stop feeling sorry for yourself, Gillian McKenzie. So Stephanie had got the project she wanted? Big deal. Since when did she let a setback get in her way of success? She hadn't become the youngest account supervisor in Rosenthal PR's history for nothing. If she wanted something in this world, she had to make it happen. Let Stephanie have her aftershave launch. Gill would throw the best damn charity party Boston ever saw and make sure Elliot Rosenthal would *have* to promote her.

Confidence renewed, she yanked open the door. Oliver Harrington, look out. Gill McKenzie was here to make some Christmas magic.

A watched water spot never grows.

Oliver Harrington stared at the spot on the ceiling in his

office. It definitely looked bigger than when he'd left last night.
Somewhere the center had a leaky pipe.

Another expense he didn't have money for. Along with a
new van and replacement glass for the broken rear windows.
His list of expenses he couldn't afford was growing as fast as
that leak.

He supposed he could always charge the plumber on his
personal card and put in for reimbursement when the center
had money. But at this rate his "get reimbursed later" list
would be the longest list of all.

Saving the world wasn't supposed to be this expensive.

Sipping his cold coffee—everything in the center seemed
to be cold these days—he turned away from the stain, back to
the mish-mash of papers on his desk. Stacks of bills, receipts
and forms warred for his attention.

Then there was Julia. The photo of his ex-fiancée beamed
up at him from the newspaper. She certainly rebounded well
after their break-up, or so it appeared by the way she clung to
her current fiancé's arm. The heir to a pharmaceutical fortune
or something like that. Wealthy, a corporate success, socially
prominent. Basically everything Oliver refused to be. The guy
looked happy enough.

Never was good enough for you, was I?

Sometimes he wondered what life would be like if he had
caved to Julia's demands and taken a job with her father. He'd
be senior vice president by now. He'd be driving a luxury
sedan instead of a broken-down pickup.

He sure as hell wouldn't be worrying about water leaks.
Crumpling the photo, he took aim for the wastebasket and
shot, missing by a foot.

"Your girlfriend's here."

The pronouncement, short and sweet, kicked all thoughts
of "what if?" aside.

"My what?" Since the disaster with Julia he had but one committed relationship, and that was with the center.

Maria Carrerra folded her arms across her body. Though only five foot one, the mother of six was by far the most formidable volunteer the center had. Her first day on the job, she'd stared down the surliest teenagers on the block with a look. Oliver knew because he'd been one of them. Her expression hadn't been unlike the one she was shooting him now. A look that said he should know what she was talking about.

"The woman from that public relations agency."

"Right." Now he remembered. "The party planner."

Peter McNabb, head of the McNabb Foundation and Oliver's chief donor, had had the misfortune of getting caught by a camera phone *in flagrante delicto* with his au pair, and so he was throwing a huge children's Christmas party at the center for damage control. Personally, Oliver hated seeing his center being used for some PR stunt, but he didn't have much choice. Not if he wanted a decent budget next year. He thought of the water stain that was no doubt expanding behind him as they spoke.

Maria, meanwhile, still stood in the doorway, giving him the look. As a volunteer she was terrific. As a secretary, not so much. "What's the matter? Go ahead and send McNabb's image-polisher in."

"I can't. She's not here."

"You just said—"

"I said she was here, meaning at the center. She went straight to the community room. Right after telling me you need to bring a tape measure with you. She's kinda bossy." A frown marred her petite features. "We're not going to have to run around doing all sorts of errands for her, are we?"

"Don't worry. I'll make sure she understands we've got other work to do besides throw this party." He might not have a choice about hosting the party, but he refused to let Peter McNabb's PR stunt take over his center.

"Good," Maria replied. "Because right now I don't think she realizes that."

The community room was in the back of the building. A refurbished cafetorium left over from when the building had been an elementary school in the 1950s, it now served as the center's main gathering space. Overall, it wasn't much. There was a stage at the far end of the room, and a battered piano tucked in the corner that Oliver had paid to have tuned last month. Several large tables were pushed against the walls, along with boxes of toys and balls of various sizes. Two of the windows had boards in them thanks to broken glass. The walls, he noticed, were looking pretty dingy, too. They could stand fresh paint. Another item for his list.

At the moment, the room played host to the preschool playgroup. Mothers gathered in folding chairs, chatting and nursing babies, while toddlers wreaked their usual havoc on the toys and snacks. Oliver spotted his appointment immediately. The willowy blond pacing the perimeter looked as out of place as a cellist at a rap competition.

He watched as her coat swayed in cadence with her steps. Cell phone stuck to her ear. Cashmere scarf. Faux-fur-trimmed hood. Stiletto-heeled boots that cost more than his paycheck. Visions of society photos danced in his head. Uptown all the way, wasn't she?

No sooner did he step toward her than a particularly havoc-wreaking boy, slightly older than the others, ran up, his mouth filled with cookies. He held out the box for Oliver to see. "Mr. Oliver! We got animal crackers!" At least that was what Oliver *thought* he said.

"Jamarcus, you get back here!" His mother, a very pregnant young woman, gestured at the boy to return. "Leave Mr. Oliver alone."

Oliver smiled. "You better listen to your mother, Jamarcus."

Realizing he was outnumbered, Jamarcus did as he was told, racing back across the room at top speed and nearly taking out the PR woman in the process.

"Whoa, pal, save the speed for the Olympics," she said, ducking out of his path. "Someone needs to cut back on the caffeine."

She moved in, hand extended. "Oliver Harrington? I'm Gill McKenzie from Rosenthal Public Relations."

For a second, Oliver lost the ability to speak. Uptown, downtown—the woman was an absolute knockout. That blond hair framed the face of an angel. A very sexy angel. With sparkling green eyes and an incredibly perfect bow of a mouth. A guy could spend hours exploring that mouth...

"Did you bring the tape measure?" he heard her ask. "I can't stay long, and I wanted to get some layout measurements. This space looks like the best area. A little dingy, but what the heck? That's what decorations are for, right?"

Had she said *dingy?* That snapped him back to reality. In a flash, everything he'd come to loathe about uptown came flying back. Gone were the longing and melancholy thoughts, wiped away by an angel-faced interloper. Didn't matter how gorgeous she was. Who did she think she was, coming here slinging insults as *his* center?

"About the space. You're going to have to move that piano, along with those tables. The toys, too. Are the kids using this room all the time? Because I'm going to need a couple days to—"

"Whoa—slow down, angel." He finally found his voice. "I'm not moving anything yet."

She blinked. A slow, deliberate action that no doubt usually had men begging to do her bidding. That it made his own insides twitch didn't help.

"Gill," she said. "My name is Gill, not Angel."

Then maybe she should *look* like a Gill. Wasn't that a man's name anyway? "My mistake, *Gill*." His annoyance was growing with each passing second. This woman was too sexy, too good-looking, too much like a society-page photo for his comfort. "But I'm still not moving a thing without knowing what's going on."

She took a moment before nodding in concession. "Sorry. I tend to get ahead of myself." Her voice had a Southern twang that didn't match her appearance. "I was thinking this room would be the best space for Mr. McNabb's Christmas party."

"You mean the center's party."

She gave him another one of those slow motion blinks.

"I was under the impression you were here to plan a Christmas party to promote the center."

"True. Mr. McNabb does want to see the McNabb Center get some well-deserved media attention, among other things."

"Among other things? Is that PR speak for creating a distraction?"

To her credit, Angel's—Gill's—expression didn't slip. "With the right message you can parlay this party into donations. People always look for causes to support come the holiday."

Which was the only reason he wasn't fighting McNabb about the event. He hated charity events, hated working them even more, but he'd sell his soul to the devil if it meant a better budget. Right now, the devil looked suspiciously angelic.

"Now," Gill continued, "about the party. Like I said, this room makes the most sense, but we're going to have to clear the space. Do you think you can have your people move the furniture?"

"I don't know. I'll have to check with my *people*."

She was trying not to roll her eyes; he could tell. He also knew he was being over the top with his attitude. He couldn't help himself. Gill, here, was pushing his buttons. He knew her type—oh, he knew her type very well. It was all about image and success. They saw his center as merely a building. They didn't see the people. Feel the connection he felt. Once they got what they needed, they walked away.

Well, if he had to court their vanity for donations, so be it. But that didn't mean he would be her lap dog, bowing to her wishes. As far as he was concerned, the people at the center were his family. And he'd never let his family be taken advantage of. His green-eyed angel had better learn the ground rules from the start.

CHAPTER TWO

GROUND rules? Gill was trying to keep her patience—really she was—but this director was making it difficult. Bad enough they were having this meeting with kids running amok, but now he wanted ground rules?

What was with all the attitude anyway? Why act as if she was the enemy? It wasn't as if she'd begged to be here.

Focus on the promotion. She took a deep breath. "What kind of ground rules?"

"First, this is a community center, not some hotel ballroom. Our job is to serve the community—which means, yes, the kids *will* be using this space right up to the party. You'll have to work around our schedule. Second, I don't have *people.* I have volunteers. They're here on their own time because they want to help the neighborhood. They aren't here to do your bidding. You want them to do something, you ask me first. If they aren't busy volunteering with the kids, then we'll see."

In other words, no help from him. She was *so* going to kill Stephanie when she got back to the office. "Anything else?"

"Yeah. I want the kids involved."

Okay, that one she could manage. "Already done. Little hard to highlight the center's work without them here."

"Not invited," he said. "Involved. There's a difference." He gestured at a group of toddlers playing some random running game that only little kids could understand. "For a lot of these kids, this is the only real Christmas celebration they'll get. I'm not going to let their holiday be hijacked, no matter how many donations this party attracts. If they get shoved aside, I won't cooperate."

Because he was the picture of cooperation at the moment. "The kids will be involved. I promise."

Gill waited while Oliver studied her face. Assessing her sincerity, no doubt. She stood her ground, even though the scrutiny made her insides jumble.

At last he nodded, apparently satisfied with what he saw. "Okay, then, why don't I show you the facilities?"

"Officially, our mission is to provide a safe alternative to life on the streets."

"And unofficially?" Gill asked. They were walking along the rear corridor of the center. She could tell from Oliver's tone of voice there were a lot of "unofficial" duties.

"Unofficially we're whatever people need us to be. Different day, different challenge."

"Sounds a lot like public relations work."

Her attempt at camaraderie didn't raise so much as a smile. "Except in this case, instead of the bottom line, people are worried about simply surviving."

"For some of my clients the bottom line *is* about survival."

"Trust me," Oliver replied with a soft snort, "it's not the same thing."

Gill said nothing. Arguing would only waste time she didn't have. Still, she didn't appreciate his dismissiveness. She worked every bit as hard as the next person, maybe harder, and just because she didn't work for a nonprofit organization, it didn't mean her work didn't count for something. It counted for a lot. It was who she was. Gill McKenzie, youngest account supervisor in Rosenthal PR's history. She'd worked hard for that title. *To become someone worth noticing.*

They rounded the corner and stopped at a set of double doors. "This is the gym," Oliver said, holding the door open.

Gill peered in, recognizing the age-old smell of sneakers and dust. Handmade posters taped to the cement wall chanted "Go Panthers!" and "Panthers Rule!"

She arched her brow. "Panthers?"

"Center's basketball team. Some of the kids are pretty good."

Pride shone in his brown eyes. It was the first time she'd seen his face show any kind of enthusiasm, and Gill had to admit the change was amazing. When she'd first met him, she'd considered Oliver Harrington handsome, but now those good-looks went deeper. His enthusiasm seemed to come from the inside and shine out, like a glow. It took what were sharp, patrician features and softened them, turning his expression youthful and engaging.

"Sounds like you all take the community part of your name seriously." That was good. She could do a lot with that line. In the back of her mind she began drafting press releases.

Oliver seemed less impressed. "We do what we can. 'Course we could always do more."

"Then Peter McNabb took the right time to get caught with his pants down, didn't he?" At Oliver's sidelong look, she added, "You get this party."

"I'm sure Mrs. McNabb feels the same way."

Actually, Gill doubted Mrs. McNabb was as upset as the board of directors, but she kept that to herself. "Seriously, if we do this party right, the center will get a ton of donations."

She purposely emphasized the word *we*. Anything to buy a little cooperation.

Oliver closed the gymnasium door. "What do you mean by 'right'?"

"Go all out. Create an event so extraordinary the media and public will have to pay attention. Give major donors a reason to attend."

"In other words, put this party on the society pages?"

Exactly. Although the way he ground out the word *society* made her regret the suggestion. "People's generosity increases after a few drinks," she reminded him. Suddenly an idea popped into her head. "We could turn the center into a Winter Wonderland, complete with snow, trees and all the rest of the holiday trimmings."

She could already picture the idea.

"Every room can focus on a different theme, with themed refreshments. Gingerbread martinis in the gymnasium, candy cane cocktails in the community room. We'll say 'The McNabb Community Center—Where Magic Happens Everywhere. Every day.' We'll be knee-deep in media coverage."

"How do the kids factor into this society wonderland?"

"Kids?"

"Yeah, the kids." He shoved his hands in his pockets, giving her a look that said she should already know what he was talking about. "You promised the kids would be involved, remember? What are they going to do? Serve the martinis?"

Ground rule number three. In her enthusiasm she had forgotten; she'd been too busy imagining decorating concepts.

It wasn't that she didn't *want* to include the kids, she simply wasn't used to kid events. That was her sister Gwen's territory. She was the maternal one in the family. Gill had always been busy working.

The scowl on Oliver's face told her that excuse wouldn't fly. "I promise the event will be kid-friendly, too," she said.

"I hope so. I was dead serious earlier. I'm not letting you shove my kids aside so a bunch of socialites can get their photo in the paper. There are plenty of other parties where they can accomplish that."

His kids? Bit possessive, wasn't he? "Even if those socialites end the night by writing you a big fat check?"

"I'd rather they write a check after walking a mile in these kids' shoes, not after sipping designer drinks. Maybe if they experienced the hardships these kids experience they'd be a little less interested in publicity."

And maybe if someone lost the chip on his shoulder he'd get a few more donations. Man, but he was difficult. Originally she'd thought putting him in a tuxedo and unleashing those good-looks on a room of society matrons would have the money rolling in. Now she wasn't so sure. With that attitude, it was a wonder he charmed any donors at all.

She glanced at her cell. The meeting was almost over. Thank goodness. She wasn't sure how much more of Oliver Harrington she could take. "Can I please see the kitchen facilities?"

"This way."

They re-entered the community room where the preschoolers were still playing their running game, although they'd broken off into smaller groups at this point. Oliver led her to a set of swinging doors. "The kitchen is right off the community room. Left over from the cafeteria days. We use it more for storage than anything. Any gatherings we host are pizza parties or pot luck."

She could tell. To call the room dated would be generous. The painted cupboards were cracked and in some cases missing hinges. Opening one, Gill found juice boxes and bulk snack packages.

"I'm sure your big-time donors would go for potato chips and apple juice," Oliver said. "I hear they're all the rage on the charity circuit these days."

"So are caterers," Gill replied, closing the refrigerator. She was starting to get seriously sick of the comments. There were charities out there that would kill for the kind of event she could provide. He could be a little more appreciative. "I'll call a couple of services I've worked with before and have them work up numbers. If that's okay with you," she added.

Oliver shrugged. "Long as my *people* aren't inconvenienced, knock yourself out."

For the first time since they'd met, Gill didn't bother disguising her eye-roll.

It was after nine o'clock when Gill finally walked through her front door. She tossed her keys in the bowl with an exhausted groan. Could today be any longer? First Stephanie's blindside this morning, followed by back-to-back meetings all day long.

Then there was Oliver Harrington and his ground rules. How was she supposed to plan a Christmas party to beat all Christmas parties with that chip he carried blocking her progress?

She was wiped. Too tired even to boil water. Thank goodness for microwave popcorn, dinner of champions.

While she waited for the kernels to pop, she unpacked her briefcase, spreading the contents across her desk. Being home didn't mean work stopped. Not if she wanted that vice presidency.

Outside, the lights on the Boston Commons sparkled and swayed like colored stars. There was a glow in the distance from the Frog Pond Pavilion. She'd heard the music from the rink when the cab dropped her off.

She loved this view. It was one of the best in the city. The first day she'd arrived in Boston, she'd walked the edge of the Common from the State House to the Central Burial Ground and fell in love with every inch. When she saw the line of brick row houses on Beacon Street—once the homes of Boston Brahmin—she knew immediately she had to live in one. It had taken eighteen months of scrimping, saving and burning the midnight oil, but she'd managed to check that goal off her list six months ago.

You've come a long way from Towering Pines and the little house on Jensen Street, she thought proudly. She wasn't poor little abandoned Gill McKenzie anymore. She was a success. Someone the world couldn't pretend didn't exist. And once she got that promotion… Well, the sky was the limit.

Of course that all depended on getting Oliver Harrington to play ball.

A beep announced dinner. How could she win the man over? she wondered as she padded back to the kitchen. There was something about the man she couldn't put her finger on—beyond the chip on his shoulder. At first glance he was arrogant and stubborn. Dedicated, though. You could see that from the way his face had lit up talking about the basketball team. You had to admire his loyalty.

Maybe that was what was throwing her. The look in his eye when he talked about the kids. The way he glowed from the inside out.

If only she could find a way to make him look that way at *her*. That was, get him to see how a successful, mind-blowing party would help his kids.

Her eyes traveled to the tabletop tree on her dining room table. Gwen had laughed when she'd sent her a photo of the tree. "Oh, my God, it's a mini-tree! How'd you get it away from its mother?" her twin had teased. Then she'd offered to send Gill what she called a "real" tree.

That was it! A tree! Gill nearly dropped the popcorn bag. Why hadn't she thought of the solution earlier? A tree was the perfect goodwill gesture. The kids would be thrilled, Oliver would see she wanted to do right by the center with this party, and maybe—just maybe—he'd give her a little more cooperation.

Grabbing her cell, she dialed Gwen's number, hoping she wasn't calling too late.

On the third ring, a familiar voice answered. "Teaberry Farms."

Warm feelings washed over her. "Hey, any idea where a girl can get a good Christmas tree?"

"Gill!" Her sister squealed with delight, making Gill smile. Gwen always sounded as if her phone calls were a lottery jackpot, even though they talked every few days. "I was just thinking of calling you."

"At this hour? I figured you and Drew would be all cozy and romantic. Don't tell me the honeymoon's over?"

"No, it's definitely still in full swing," her sister replied, almost dreamily. "Drew's at the airport getting Brody. He's in for Christmas break."

"I can't believe you have a college-age stepson. How is Mr. UCLA doing, anyway? Still planning to be the next big movie director?"

"Depends on who you ask. He says great. His father thinks he spends too much time enjoying himself and not enough time in the library."

"Typical student."

"And he's been talking a lot about some girl named Susan."

"Is it serious?"

"Doubt it. Last month it was Jessica."

"Don't worry, he'll settle down eventually. Look at his father." Drew Teaberry had been quite the playboy until he'd met Gwen. Now he was a doting father and husband.

"True. Drew just hopes he doesn't take as long as he did to smarten up. How about you? Any irons in the fire?"

Gill, who was emptying the popcorn into a bowl, laughed. She knew what kind of irons Gwen meant. They had this same conversation at least once a month. The problem with her twin was that Gwen had an incurable romantic streak, and marriage to the man of her dreams had only made it worse.

"When would I have time to meet anyone? Between meetings? I've been working nonstop."

"But it's Christmas."

"Like that makes a difference in the PR industry."

"Don't you want someone to cuddle up with under the Christmas tree? Or to get trapped under the mistletoe with?"

"The only thing I want for Christmas is promotion to vice president. Which," she tossed a kernel in the air and caught it in her mouth "got a little harder, thanks to Stephanie DeWitt."

Briefly she explained how she'd lost the Remaillard account and ended up working on the Christmas party.

"Talk about passive-aggressive," Gwen said when she was done. "I can't believe your boss buys her act."

"Worse, the guy I'm supposed to work with, Oliver Harrington, has major attitude issues. He absolutely hates the idea of throwing this party and refuses to cooperate."

"Sounds like a piece of work."

"Oh, he is." Gill flopped on the sofa. "Sad thing is, without the superiority complex he'd probably be a nice guy. He's certainly dedicated to the center. I'm not certain, but I think he might actually live there."

"A workaholic? Sounds like you two have something in common."

"Hardy, har-har." She wasn't that big a workaholic. Just goal-oriented. "I just wish I knew what made him so angry. I mean, I get the whole frustrated nonprofit thing, but his attitude goes a lot deeper."

"Maybe he got burned once upon a time by some big bad donor?"

"He did say they were having budget issues. And Peter McNabb hasn't exactly been paying attention to the center the past few years." She tossed another piece of popcorn in the air. "Except for a little while, he acted more like he was mad at me personally, and for the life of me I don't know what I did."

"Maybe you look like his ex-wife?"

"You're a laugh riot tonight, sis. Maybe you ought to chuck the Christmas tree business for standup comedy."

"And *you* need some sleep. You always get cranky when you're tired. Sounds like this guy's gotten under your skin."

"More like *on* my skin, like a big old rash. I can tell right now he's going to give me a hard time with this whole project."

"You can always quit and join us down here, selling Christmas trees."

"I'm sure Drew would love that."

"Seriously, why not visit for the weekend? Claire would love to see her Aunt Gilly. Lord knows we could use the help. From the buzz in town, this might be our busiest year yet."

"Everyone's looking for a piece of Teaberry magic," Gill joked. "Hoping to have their Christmas wish granted."

"Why not? It worked for me and Drew," Gill replied.

No, thought Gwen, love, timing and effort had worked for them. Whatever magic Gwen and Drew had found, they'd made it for themselves. They still made magic. Gill didn't think she'd ever seen two people more in love or more happy. As if they'd been waiting their whole lives to find each other.

Suddenly a heavy feeling settled in the pit of her stomach. Guess popcorn for dinner wasn't a good idea after all.

"I'd love to see you guys, but with this last-minute project I'm swamped. Plus, if I have any hope of getting this promotion...."

"Say no more. I understand," Gwen replied. "That's the price I pay for having a high-powered executive for a sister."

"I'm not a high-powered executive yet."

"You will be. You always succeed when you put your mind to something. Remember when Mr. Delphino said he didn't think you could handle advanced chemistry?"

"I remember studying my butt off day and night."

"Finishing with the highest grade in the class. You make things happen, Gill."

Yes, she did. That was how it had always been. Gwen was the romantic dreamer; Gill was the doer. Not that she'd had much of choice, what with their mother working day and night, and dear old Dad... Well, better to take a page from his book and wipe him from her memory.

Her stomach got a little heavier.

"Too bad you won't put that mind to making something happen in your personal life," Gwen continued.

Back to that, were they? Her sister could be a real broken record sometimes. Gill told her as much.

"Can't help it. I want you to be as happy as Drew and I are."

"I *am* happy. I have the career I always wanted, a great apartment, you guys... What more could I want?"

"You want the long or the short list?"

"Neither, thank you. What I really need is a favor." Clearing her throat, she set down the popcorn and sat up a little straighter. "I need you to ship a little Teaberry magic up north."

"You need a Christmas tree?"

"Not *just* a Christmas tree. The most amazing Christmas tree you've got." She started explaining, and Gwen quickly caught on to her plan. Score one for the twin connection. By the time the call ended they'd come up with one amazing tree.

Gill hung up feeling a little better. Talking to Gwen never failed to cheer her up.

But as she lay back and studied the Christmas lights on her mini-tree it wasn't her sister she was thinking about. It was Oliver Harrington. No way he'd be able to keep that chip on his shoulder now. He was going to be blown away.

She couldn't wait.

CHAPTER THREE

"WE'RE low on lights."

Gill squinted up at the decorator standing on the scaffolding.

"Are you sure this is all we can use?" he asked.

"Positive. I don't want to take a chance on blowing any circuits." Further incurring Oliver's wrath. "Lord knows when they last upgraded their electrical system."

Gill had expected quite a different reaction from him when he came in today. She'd been disappointed to find him out this morning, but Maria had said he'd spent the last two days dealing with a plumbing crisis and was home catching some much needed sleep.

It surprised her how *off* the center felt without him. There was an emptiness in the air. Not that she missed him. She was simply aware of his absence.

On the other hand, having him gone made installing the tree easier. She'd be able to surprise him with it fully decorated. Why impressing him had become so important she wasn't sure, other than knowing his cooperation would make her job easier. His disapproval was so damn frustrating. The way he glared at her, as if she was the enemy in high heels.

"Done!" the decorator hollered down. "I still think we need more lights…"

"No, it's perfect."

Gwen and Drew had outdone themselves. Decked from trunk to tip with ribbons and poinsettias, the tree was a magnificent sight of red and gold. And even without a lot of lights the tree sparkled. The crystal decorations caught the light from the windows, creating their own twinkling reflection. Gill got a giddy shiver. She couldn't wait for the rest of the center to see it. *For Oliver to see it.*

Gwen's note was clipped to her clipboard.

Here's your tree, Sis. May you get the Christmas magic you deserve.

Leave it to her sister to turn a business transaction whimsical. Still, if by "magic" she meant the tree would bring Oliver's goodwill and cooperation, then Gill would take it.

"Wow!" Maria's voice sounded behind her. "So this is why you needed to get in here at the crack of dawn. That thing looks bigger than the one at City Hall."

"Being inside makes it look bigger."

"Maybe. It looks huge. Smells good, too."

"Doesn't it?" A fresh pine scent filled the community room. If Gill closed her eyes she could picture Christmas morning. Claire, her niece, tearing open presents with toddler enthusiasm. Brody engrossed in the latest video game. Gwen and Drew cuddling on the sofa. Her sitting by the fire.

Alone.

A sudden wave of longing swept over her, not unlike the emptiness that filled the center. Gill frowned. This was because of Gwen's note and her romanticism. They'd put weird thoughts into her head.

"Looks like they'll finish decorating before Oliver returns. Do you think he'll be surprised?" she asked Maria.

Odd how he was her next thought. On the other hand, why wouldn't he be? She'd gotten this tree for him. That was, to win him over.

"He'll be something, that's for sure," the volunteer replied.

"There are matching decorations for the foyer and the rest of the building, too. Enough to deck out the whole place."

"Wow."

Maria sounded blown away. Exactly the reaction Gill had hoped for. Now just let Oliver have the same reaction when he arrived later. Absentmindedly she played with the end of a branch. "Christmas magic, do your stuff," she murmured.

"What the hell—?"

At the sound of Oliver's voice, she whirled around with a grin. "Surprise!"

Oliver stood like a guardian sentinel in the doorway. The atmosphere, she noticed, had returned to normal with his arrival. "What is *that?*" he asked.

She grinned wider. "The center's Christmas tree. What do you think?"

He set down the bags of supplies he'd been carrying and stepped closer. Unlike their last meeting, when he'd been in corduroys and a sweater, today he was dressed for hard labor. His jeans were paint-splattered and worn, as was his heavy zippered sweatshirt and a flannel shirt. A faded Red Sox cap topped his head. Normally Gill didn't get the whole construction worker fascination, but now seeing Oliver, she kind of understood better.

"I thought you went home to sleep," Maria commented.

"I did. Then I went to the hardware store for paint. Thought I'd paint the storage room while the center was slow." While he talked, his eyes took in everything. The ladders, the decorators, the piles of garlands waiting to be hung. Gill was practically bouncing in her shoes, waiting for his response. "This tree looks like it came from a decorating magazine."

"Isn't it fantastic?" She had to fight to keep from giggling with enthusiasm. "The same decorators did the tree at the Governor's house." She cradled one of the glass globes. "Look! Lalique."

"Lalique crystal?"

"I know what you're thinking." She'd already anticipated the argument. "But this won't impact the budget a bit. Everything you see has been donated by Teaberry Farms—finest Christmas trees in West Virginia." She let the globe rest among the branches. "Originally Gwen and I discussed just the tree, but then Drew got involved and insisted on the decorations and the trimmings, too."

"Drew?" Oliver repeated. "As in Drew Teaberry? From Teaberry Industries?"

"Uh-huh. He's married to my sister Gwen. I had the tree shipped up earlier this week And before you ask, yes, I got the necessary permits. Everything is legal and to code."

"I'm sure it is," he said.

"So what do you think?"

Thus far he hadn't shown any reaction all, other than to stare and walk back and forth. Gill tried studying his profile, but his handsome features were unreadable. She glanced at Maria, only to get an equally cryptic shrug.

"Twenty feet of blue spruce," she continued, filling the silence. "I wasn't sure of the exact ceiling measurements, so I erred on the side of caution. From the looks of things..." she craned her neck upward "...I could have gone another five or six feet."

Still nothing. Her spirits flagged. What now? She'd just presented him with a stunning, one-of-kind designer tree and trimmings free of charge. Where was the happiness? The gratitude? The appreciation?

"Usually we get our tree from the vendor up the street," he replied finally.

"If you're concerned about taking business away from the neighborhood, we can make a donation."

"What about the kids? They were supposed to make decorations today. What happened to keeping them involved?"

"They can be involved in something else. Trust me, when they see this tree they won't mind."

"That's another thing. How am I supposed to explain where all this came from?" He waved his arm across the decorations.

"How about Santa's workshop?"

"I'm serious."

So was she. Not to mention increasingly frustrated. "For goodness' sake, it's a Christmas tree. Why are you acting like I kicked a puppy?"

He turned, giving her full view of his annoyed expression. "A lot of these kids will be lucky if they get a handful of gifts, and most of those will be donated. What are they going to think when they see a tree with decorations that cost more than their parents will make in a year?"

Gill bit her lip. She hadn't thought about that point, although the solution seemed simple enough. "Tell them the truth. The tree was a generous donation."

"Sure. Right after I tell them I had to spend the money for the new ping-pong table on plumbing supplies. I'll say 'Hey, kids, no ping-pong, but good news—we got a tree.'"

Oh, for crying out loud. Was there no pleasing this guy? "You know," she said, crossing her arms, "Most people in your shoes would say thank you when presented with a gift like this."

"Really? And what would you know about what people 'in my shoes' would say?"

More than you know, Gill wanted to reply. She knew exactly what it felt like to look in someone's window and see the Christmas you couldn't have. "I'm only trying to give the kids something special."

"Don't you mean show off? Is that what people in *your shoes* do?"

How dared—? She turned so Oliver couldn't see the hurt and anger in her eyes. Since the moment they'd met, Oliver had acted as if she was the enemy. All she wanted was to do a good job. What had she done to make this man dislike her so much?

Well, she was done trying to win him over. The tree was amazing, and if he was too stubborn to appreciate her efforts, or even to show a modicum of gratitude—well, then he could simply go to blazes. She didn't care anymore.

"We're done!" the decorator called down. "Do you want to light her up and see what she looks like?"

"Ask Mr. Harrington," she called back. "It's his electrical system."

She gathered her coat and belongings, no longer able to stand the stiff, unfriendly atmosphere. "Tell you what," she snapped. "If you don't like the tree, take it down. Better yet, why don't you stick it—?"

Her voice cracked, preventing her from finishing the sentence. Didn't matter; he'd get the idea. "It can keep the other stick that's up there company."

CHAPTER FOUR

"SELF-RIGHTEOUS, stubborn, obnoxious..." Gill ran out of adjectives before she reached the sidewalk. What was this man's problem? She got him a one-of-a-kind tree half the city—strike that, the *whole* city—would kill for, and he was insulted? Did he hate Christmas?

Or just hate her?

She stomped down the front steps, blaming the harsh December air for the moisture rimming her eyes. She'd been so certain he'd like the tree; so excited to show him.

"Stupid Christmas party," she muttered, swiping at her cheeks. Stupid Oliver Harrington and his stupid brown eyes and broad shoulders. She wished she'd never met the man.

Oliver and Maria stood listening to the silence left in the wake of Gill's door slam. "You know," Maria said, "sometimes you can be a real jerk."

He certainly felt like one right now.

"She thought she was doing something nice," Maria continued. "And you come in here acting like she stole all your money or something. What's wrong with you?"

He wished he knew. He'd overreacted for sure. When he saw the tree, big and beautiful, unlike anything he could ever afford, and Gill standing by its branches, her angelic face all excited, looking like a magazine advertisement, he'd lost it. Big-time.

He thought of the way Gill's face had crumpled at his reaction. Like a five-year-old being told there was no Santa Claus. She'd tried to hide it, but he'd caught the moisture in her eyes. The way her lower lip had trembled with disappointment.

Maria was right. He was a jerk.

She might as well kiss that promotion goodbye right now. If she couldn't handle a simple Christmas party, how on earth was Elliot going to see her as vice president material? So much for Teaberry magic. Stupid tree blew up in her face.

The look on Oliver's face... She couldn't shake the image. He'd looked so...angry. No, not angry. Horrified. *Face it, Gillian. The guy simply doesn't like you.*

Her breath made a white puff as she sighed. She'd had it all planned. She'd create this magical tree, unlike anything the kids at the center had ever seen, beautiful and breathtaking and beyond their wildest imaginations. Oliver would see how much she wanted to help the center and, impressed, he'd be thrilled to work with her. Instead, she was now more on his bad side than ever.

Okay, so maybe she *was* showing off a little, like Oliver had said. Maybe she *could* have toned things down a bit. Then again, why? The tree was absolutely gorgeous. Leave it to Oliver Harrington to prefer paper chain garlands and popsicle stick ornaments over Lalique crystal.

For the life of her, she didn't know why his disapproval bothered her so much. In the larger scheme of things, whether he liked the tree or not didn't matter. Neither did his cooperation. As long as she made Peter McNabb look good in the press.

So why was she so determined to dazzle Oliver?

* * *

You're jealous of a tree. It was true. In a million years Oliver couldn't give the center a tree like this, and Gill McKenzie had done it with one simple phone call. To her millionaire brother-in-law to boot.

"So what are you going to do?" Maria asked.

"I don't know."

"Here's an idea. How about you apologize?"

Yeah, he owed Gill at least that. How would she know the tree would hit such a strong nerve?

Or that her appearance would be part of the problem?

Therein lay the crux of the matter. Gill McKenzie was uptown, upscale, and everything else he wasn't. Would never be.

She's not Julia.

No, but she was a walking reminder of everything Julia had chosen when she'd walked out on him.

Still, that was no reason to take his frustration out on the woman.

On the other hand, there was no reason for him to be so worried about her feelings, either. It wasn't as if they would have a relationship beyond this party, right? In fact, *relationship* wasn't even the right word, since that implied something long-lasting. Once this party debacle was over she would head back uptown, never to be seen again.

Still… Those trembling lips flashed in front of his eyes.

He should definitely apologize.

Her surroundings began to change, morphing from slightly rundown to the bland brick buildings of a housing project. So intent had Gill been on fuming, she hadn't realized she'd walked to the center of the neighborhood. Because it was the middle of a work day, the area was quiet. A pair of women bundled in heavy coats waited at the bus stop. One held the hand of a little boy, his face hidden by his bulky hood. He had some type of plastic toy in his hand.

Glancing up at the apartment windows, she saw collections of lights and various decorations. Nothing fancy. Certainly nothing like her tree. One window toward the end of the building was covered with paper snowflakes. Despite her bad mood, Gill couldn't help smiling, thinking how she and Gwen had used to do the same thing. They hadn't had a lot as kids. They hadn't been as badly off as some of these families, but they'd done their fair share of going without. Every Christmas she and Gwen would deck their house with pictures and cut-out snowflakes. Their mother would hang up each and every one as if they were precious works of art. Same with those God-awful decorations they'd made at school. Their tree would be literally covered with sparkly pieces of cardboard and popsicle sticks. It wouldn't have won any decorating awards, but it had been erected with love.

Her smile faded.

Like the tree Oliver had planned for the center.

"Wow!"

"It's got to be like a hundred feet tall!"

"Is it real?"

"Can we touch it?"

The kids in the after-school program peppered Oliver with question after question, barely waiting for an answer before asking another. They loved the tree—couldn't stop talking about how awesome and amazing it was. Every comment was a little "I told you so" kick to the stomach.

"Looks like Gill was right," Maria said, adding to the attack. "The kids are blown away."

"I noticed." Guilt made his stomach ache worse.

"Did you call her and apologize?"

"Her office said she was out." Twice. He'd tried calling her cell phone, too, with no luck. She had either turned it off or she was ignoring his calls. He told himself the unsettled feeling in his stomach was simply eagerness to clear the air, nothing more. "I'll try again later, after the kids settle down."

"Did Santa bring the tree?"

Looking down, he saw Becky, one of the younger girls in the program, her brown eyes wide with curiosity.

"How'd he fit it in the sleigh?"

"You'd be surprised at what those elves can do," a familiar voice replied.

Like a dancer hearing her cue, in waltzed Gill, carrying a tabletop tree. Her cheeks were bright pink, her hair tussled and windblown. She wore a smile so bright that Oliver's first thought was that she outshone the tree.

"Hey," she continued, "they pack for an entire Christmas Eve in one trip. A tree is nothing."

"What's that?" Becky asked, pointing to the tree in Gill's hand.

"Oh, this? This is a mini-tree. You can't have an enchanted forest without a lot of trees, right?"

"What's enchanted mean?"

"It means magical," Gill replied.

Carlos DeGarza, the boy standing behind Becky, scoffed. "There's no such thing as a magical Christmas tree."

Gill eyed him. "You sure?"

"I ain't seen one."

"You've never seen an elephant in your backyard, either. Doesn't mean they don't exist."

"I saw an elephant at the zoo," Becky said.

"Well, this tree is from where I grew up," Gill said. "And in my hometown people believe in magical trees all the time."

"They do?"

"Uh-huh."

She glanced at Oliver, hesitation in her eyes, and Oliver felt a stab of guilt, knowing it was his attitude that had put it there. With a nod, he encouraged her to continue. He had to admit he was as curious as the kids to hear what she was going to say. This young woman in front of him, talking about magical Christmas trees, was barely recognizable as the glossy Gill McKenzie of this morning.

Gill moved over to the tree and plucked a couple of pine needles. "This isn't just *any* tree. This is a Teaberry tree."

"So?" Carlos asked.

"So," she answered, "for as long as I can remember people have believed if you touch the branch of a Teaberry tree and make a wish, the wish will come true."

Carlos, junior cynic that he was, frowned. "No way. That's stupid."

Clearly Becky didn't think so. Her eyes, impossible to believe, were larger than ever. "Do they?"

"Sometimes," Gill replied, casting a quick glance in Oliver's direction. "But only if the person really *wants* the wish to come true."

Squatting down to the kids' eye level, she held out the needles, drawing Oliver and the kids further into her orbit. "See, I have a theory. I think the real magic is inside us. It's not the tree or the actual wishing, it's what we do with the wish. I think the tree knows this and rewards the people who do the work."

"Like doing your homework so you do good in school?" Becky piped in.

"Exactly. Or practicing your hook shot so you make the high school basketball team."

"I have a hook shot," Carlos said. He'd been won over.

"But what are the little trees for?" Becky asked.

"Like I said, this tree is part of an enchanted forest."

"But it doesn't have any decorations," said a voice from the back. Oliver recognized it as Dontrell, one of the older boys.

Gill smiled. Her eyes grew almost as wide as Becky's. "Then I guess we better do something about that. Oliver said you guys were going to make Christmas decorations today, right?"

The little girl looked at Oliver, as if to ask. He nodded. "If you want to."

"You better make a lot, then," Gill told them. "I've got a few dozen more mini-trees on their way. Enough for everyone to have their own to decorate."

She might as well have announced Santa had arrived. The center erupted with murmurs of enthusiasm. "Cool. Do we get to keep them?" someone asked.

Gill smiled. "Absolutely. You can bring them home Christmas Eve."

"Will they be magical, too?" Becky asked.

"Maybe," she replied, giving the girl's braids a tug. "Maybe…"

Oliver watched as the kids gathered around Gill, peppering her with the same excited questions they'd asked him a short time before. To her credit, she fielded each and every one with an enthusiasm to match. It was impressive to see. For an uptown girl she was more comfortable with kids than he'd expected.

"Looks like you owe her more than a simple apology," he heard Maria murmur in his ear.

Unable to tear his gaze away from Gill's enthusiastic face, he nodded. "Yeah," he replied. "I think I do."

CHAPTER FIVE

As PROMISED, the trees arrived, and the kids had a blast bickering over which tree would be "theirs." Gill watched the chaos, feeling pretty darn good about her problem-solving skills. The kids were happy. Peter McNabb would be happy.

And Oliver was happy. She looked over at how he was smiling at the kids and felt a surge of satisfaction.

He must have felt her stare, for he suddenly turned his smile in her direction. Gill's insides tumbled. She'd never noticed before, but his eyes had green-gold flecks in them. And dimples. He had dimples. Made her wonder what else she missed.

Picking up one of the leftover mini-trees, she headed in his direction.

"That a peace offering?" he asked, seeing what she carried.

"Santa had room for one more. Looks like it might be the runt of the litter, though."

"It's not such a bad little tree."

Her insides jumbled a wee bit more. Maybe he wasn't such an ogre after all.

Turning to the craziness on the other side of the room, she said, "Looks like the kids liked my idea." She couldn't help the smug smile tugging the corners of her mouth. "Not to mention my tree."

"Yeah, about that… I, um…" With his free hand, he rubbed the back of his neck. From his sheepish expression, and the way he suddenly averted his eyes, Gill suspected admitting a mistake wasn't something he did much of. "I might have overreacted a bit."

Gill couldn't help herself. "A bit?"

"Maybe more than a bit. I saw the tree and the decorations and I… Well, it's complicated."

"I understand."

"You do?"

Gill nodded. "Took me a few minutes—or blocks, as the case may be—but, yeah, I do. You were looking out for the kids. You didn't want them to get the wrong idea. And maybe…"

She brushed her hand over the bottom branch of Oliver's tree, studying the needles that stuck to her palm. Admitting she was wrong wasn't something *she* did well, either. "Maybe I got a bit carried away, too."

"A bit?"

"Point taken. Though you've got to admit the tree *is* pretty amazing."

"Breathtaking," Oliver replied, catching her gaze.

All of sudden the air in the center grew close, and for a moment it was as if he meant her, not the tree. A heat rose up inside her, starting somewhere low and feminine, and moving through her limbs and chest until she was warm and melty all over.

Oliver turned his attention back to the kids, and the sensation vanished as quickly as it appeared. "So," he said clearing his throat, "magical Teaberry trees, huh?"

She'd surprised herself with the tale. Normally she wasn't

the gather-round-for a-story type, but for some reason the words had seemed to pour out easily today. "What can I say? I'm from the South. We're full of rural legends. I grew up on that one. My sister Gwen believes it wholeheartedly." Too wholeheartedly, maybe, she added, thinking about the note in her pocket.

"But you don't."

A statement rather than a question. Gill appreciated the understanding. "I believe what I told the kids—people make their own magic. You want something in this life, you have to make it happen."

She realized Oliver was looking at her again, with an odd glint in his eye. "Is that experience talking?"

"You bet."

"Hmmm." In his response, Gill found a kind of kinship, a bond they'd missed during their other meetings. "Yet here you are surrounded by Teaberry trees and talking magic. Funny how home has a way of pulling people back."

"A onetime occurrence, I assure you." Perhaps it was the way Oliver said it, but hearing the word *home* brought on a restlessness she couldn't identify. As if something was eating away at the periphery of her life's plan. She'd felt the same feeling earlier in the day, when setting up the tree. "I made up my mind a long time ago to get as far away from Towering Pines as possible. If Gwen wasn't there, I'd never go back."

"Onward and upward, huh?" There was an edge to his voice she couldn't identify.

"Something like that."

Carlos, Becky and a few other kids were rooting around the greenery still on the floor, picking up the scraps of bunting the decorators had left behind. Gill watched, marveling at their enthusiasm. Did kids always find fun in everything?

"You didn't let the decorators do the windows and the other

decorations," she noted to Oliver. "Is that because you don't want to?"

"No, I told them I'd do the decorating myself. After our little…" he cleared his throat "…discussion, I got the impression they weren't keen on sticking around with a guy who had a stick up his…" He looked away, but not before Gill caught the color flooding his cheeks.

She felt her own cheeks growing warm, too. "I probably overstepped a little there. Though you have to admit you have had a bit of a—"

"Stick?"

"I was going to say chip."

Their eyes met, and in spite of themselves they both grinned. "Think we can start over?" Gill asked. "Call a truce?"

Oliver looked at the kids, who were still laughing and scrounging among the pine boughs. "We could try."

With that, he slipped his fingers around hers to seal the deal. Their hands, Gill couldn't but notice, fit together perfectly. The melty sensation began anew.

"What's this?" Carlos hollered.

He ran up holding a sprig of green and white berries he'd dug from amid the branches. The stem had a red bow tied to it. The minute she saw what he had in his hand, Gill felt her cheeks grow red again. *Gwen, I'm going to kill you….*

"Can you eat the berries?"

Oliver was the first of them to recover, releasing Gill's hand and snatching the twig from the boy. "You do and you'll get sick. This is mistletoe."

"If you don't eat it, what *do* you do?"

"You hang it," Gill explained. "Then, if you're standing under it with a girl at Christmas time, you're supposed to kiss her."

"And she can't slap you?"

"No," Oliver chuckled. "She can't."

"Sweet! Where you gonna hang it?" Carlos asked. You could see from the glint in his eye he was already making plans to drag some unsuspecting girl or girls underneath.

"We'll see, Carlos. Maria's passing out art supplies. You better go get yours." He waited until the boy had sprinted back to the crowd before holding the sprig up for review. "Mistletoe? Let me guess. Your sister believes in its magical powers, too. Or is this your doing?"

Her cheeks hotter than Hades, Gill shook her head. And not because when Oliver held it up she thought about getting stuck beneath the branch with him. "She must have slipped it into the order as her way of creating more Christmas magic."

"Well, from the sounds of things Carlos is thinking of making his own."

"Are you going to hang it up?"

Oliver shrugged. "I don't know," he replied, catching her eye. "What do you think?"

Again came the melting sensation. What was wrong with her? Ever since she'd returned to the center she'd been having completely uncharacteristic reactions. Since when did she get all weak-kneed around a male colleague? Men didn't fit into her eighty-hour work week—at least not in traditional, dating members of the opposite sex terms. So why was she reacting like a teenage girl every time Oliver so much as looked in her direction this afternoon?

Figuring the best solution would be distance, she snatched a bough from the ground. "What I think is that I should get this garland hung before the kids trample everything."

For the next few hours she immersed herself in hanging greenery and draping bunting. Her conscience nagged that she should be back at the office tending to other clients. Except, she argued with herself, she was already dressed for manual labor, so it made sense to do all the decorating in one day rather than make a second trip. Besides, the enchanted forest was her vision. She didn't want to trust the decorations to someone else.

At least that was the argument she made to herself. It was about doing this party right.

It had nothing to do with the man painting the supply room nearby.

She was tacking up the last piece of garland around the community room door when the alarm on her cell rang, indicating it was time for her Pilates class. It couldn't be six o'clock already, could it?

Sure enough, checking the screen, she saw she'd shot the entire day.

"Time has a way of getting away from you at this place, doesn't it?" Oliver remarked, wiping his hands on a cloth in the doorway. Flecks of white decorated his hat brim and the shoulders of his flannel shirt. His face was flushed, no doubt from working in a small space. Manual labor looked good on him, thought Gill. Really good.

So much for distance curing her fixation.

"Happens to me all the time," he continued. "Some days I wonder if I wouldn't be better off setting up a cot in my office."

"Some days I wonder why you haven't," Maria remarked, shrugging into her coat. "I've got to go home and remind my teenagers what I look like. The decorations look amazing, Gill. For what it's worth, I told Grinchy here there was nothing wrong with your original tree."

Red crept into Oliver's cheeks. "I've already apologized for my behavior."

"Well, it wouldn't hurt for you to apologize again," she

called over her shoulder. "You could use the practice." With that, the front door shut, leaving Gill and Oliver.

Alone.

CHAPTER SIX

OLIVER immediately ducked his head, rubbing the back of his neck. "She, uh, doesn't cut me a lot of slack."

"She certainly speaks her mind," Gill replied.

"That she does."

They stood in awkward silence, with each smiling at the other like mute statues. Something between them had shifted since this morning's shouting match. Sure, Oliver had apologized, but there was more. Gill felt as if she was seeing him in a different light. He was in his element. That was it. She'd spent the afternoon watching him interact with the kids. No wonder he seemed so appealing.

The kids weren't here now, though. And the atmosphere still felt charged between them.

"I should head back downtown," she said, aware that she'd made the same comment three hours earlier.

"Back to the grind?"

"I think I've already blown the day. I'll probably go home and catch up on some e-mails from there." She headed toward the piano where she'd draped her coat and portfolio. The mistletoe lay next to her belongings. With a chuckle, she held it up. "Decided against Carlos' plan after all?"

"No, I'm going to hang the branch; I just thought I'd wait until Carlos and the girls were gone to keep the kissing to a minimum. Something tells me I'm going to have to keep an eye on him."

"Boys will be boys." She twirled Gwen's surprise between her fingers, mentally shaking her head at her sister's romanticism.

"Although nothing says I can't make carrying out his plans a little more difficult." Near the stage there was a display board, filled with notices and announcements. Oliver crossed the room and removed a pushpin from one of the flyers.

"Come here," he said.

Gill obeyed, joining him under the main entrance. Wordlessly, he slipped the mistletoe branch from her hand and, using the pin, suspended the ribbon from the top of the frame.

"There," he said with a satisfied voice. "Now I can watch the action from all angles."

"Smart," Gill remarked, her eyes on the tiny green branch. "If Operation Mistletoe gets out of hand—"

"I can nip it in the bud."

They lowered their gazes at the same time, coming eye to eye.

The air stilled. Or maybe just Gill's breathing. Either way, she was suddenly overwhelmed by how silent and close the room felt. Oliver's gaze lowered to her mouth and then moved back. The flannel of his shirt brushed against the edge of her jacket. Had they always been standing so close?

Neither moved. There was paint in Oliver's hair, Gill noticed. And on his face. Freckle-size white spots splattered across the bridge of his nose. She had the sudden urge to wipe them away with her hand. Then comb her fingers through his light brown hair...

Suddenly Oliver was speaking, "Let me lock up and I'll

walk you to your car. You shouldn't be walking the streets alone in the dark."

"That's all right." In the back of her mind she wanted to note that he'd let Maria walk alone, but couldn't. "I'll call a cab."

"A taxi will take forever at rush hour—if it bothers to come to this neighborhood at all. Why don't I drive you?"

"I—I—" With him standing so near, her brain had trouble working right. Of course she could step back, but, as twice before, her feet simply wouldn't move. "I don't want to put you out," she finally managed to say.

"Consider the ride my second apology."

If she hadn't been standing a hair's width from the man she'd have told him no, a ride wasn't necessary. But he *was* standing that close, and the idea of trading that proximity for a ride in a cold, dark cab all of a sudden seemed quite foolish. "If you don't mind…"

He smiled. "I'll get my jacket and keys."

"Meanwhile, while I'm spending all this effort selling the magazine on an article, the client decides she needs to 'liven up' her image, and so when the photographer arrives at her office she's wearing a leather suit and lace bustier."

"Wait—I thought you said the client was in her early sixties?"

"I did."

"Whoa!"

"Whoa, indeed," Gill replied. "Worse yet, the article was highlighting her conservative family values."

Oliver coughed. "Nice. After that, Peter McNabb must be a piece of cake."

"Believe me, he is."

She watched as Oliver topped off her green tea. What was

she doing? This was supposed to be a simple ride home. How had she ended up in a hole-in-the-wall Chinese restaurant in an area of Chinatown she'd never known existed?

It had all started when they'd got into Oliver's truck. The last time she'd been in a pickup truck was in high school, when Bill Travers had driven her to homecoming. As she'd slid into the passenger seat of Oliver's vehicle she'd been struck by how small and dark the space was. She didn't remember Billy's truck feeling so…so…intimate. She'd been in the middle of buckling her seat belt, and hoping the cold would kill the weird sensation, when her stomach had chosen that moment to growl. Loudly.

Oliver had heard, and asked when she'd last eaten.

"Breakfast," she'd confessed. After that, she'd been too preoccupied for food.

"Me, too," Oliver had replied as he'd started the engine. "I meant to go out and grab a bite, but I kept getting distracted."

By her and her trees.

Gill had assumed the exchange marked the end of the conversation, but then her stomach had continued to rumble. About a block into the drive, during which her stomach had growled at least three or four times, Oliver had turned and looked at her. "You like Chinese?"

Gill had nodded. Chinese was her favorite.

"There's a place not far from here that serves a mean Kung Pao Chicken. How about we grab some?"

Common sense had told her to say no. Her phone was full of e-mails waiting for her answer. Plus she should call Gwen, to let her know how the kids had loved the tree.

But she'd been sitting in Oliver's dimly lit truck, still in close enough proximity that the mistletoe's spell hadn't worn off, and she'd said yes instead. It would be like a meeting, she'd rationalized. They could talk about the party and what she envisioned for publicity.

Now, an hour later, they were sitting in the back of a half-filled restaurant, having talked about everything *but* Peter McNabb's party until now, and Gill was wondering once again how and when things between them had shifted so dramatically.

She sipped her tea, noticing Oliver was studying her mouth again. Her mind flashed to that moment under the mistletoe. The spell continued to linger in the air between them, making every action seem slow-eyed and deliberate. Gwen, if she were here, would be having a field-day with the knowledge.

Gill tried to think of the last time she'd found a man so attractive. The answer failed her. Then again, who had time for dating when building a career? Going solo was the trade-off you made for success. Besides, she wasn't interested in dating.

Not that this was a date anyway. Even if the restaurant's dim lighting and soft music *were* made for romance.

"Hey, where'd you go?" Oliver called to her from the other side of the table. "You faded off there for a moment," he said.

"Sorry. I was thinking about work." The answer was half-true, anyway. "I'm going to have a lot of work to make up tomorrow."

"That your hint that you want to leave?"

"No, not yet." What was she doing? He'd given her the perfect out, and she was dragging her feet. "I'm enjoying myself."

"Me, too," he replied, spearing a piece of broccoli as he spoke. "Nice change of pace, eating Chinese food that's not from a carton."

"Tell me about it. The take-out guy in my neighborhood knows me by name."

"I hear that's a hazard of being a workaholic."

"Says the man who stayed up late repairing drywall," she remarked, accepting the plate of pork fried rice he was handing her.

"Point taken," he replied. "Though in my case I kind of have to. The center's budget doesn't exactly allow for delegating. Or hiring a repairman, for that matter." He took a bite of chicken, chewing it thoughtfully. "What's your excuse?"

"Love of hard work. I like my job. I like making things happen."

"Do you? Make things happen?"

She returned his grin. "All the time."

Before either of them could continue the waitress arrived with the bill and customary fortune cookies. Oliver reached into his back pocket for his wallet. "Let me," she said. "We'll call it a business expense."

He regarded her with a tilt of his head. "Is that what this was? Business?"

"Everything's business in my life," she replied.

The answer earned her a strangely shadowed look that she couldn't decipher. Surely he wasn't disappointed by her response? Did he think this dinner was something more? Or was that wishful thinking on her part?

No, not wishful thinking. She wasn't looking for more in her life than what she already had, thank you very much.

Cutting off her circular thoughts, she proffered the plate of cookies instead. "Go ahead—you choose first. You have to share what fortune you get, though."

"Very well." He broke the cookie open, revealing the thin white strip. "'What you've been looking for will soon be yours.' Hope that means I'm getting a new van."

"Or a plumbing credit," Gill said.

"Now, *that* would be a good fortune," he replied, popping half the cookie in his mouth. When Gill didn't crack hers open, he gestured with his head. "Your turn. Unless you're afraid the magic tree will get jealous?"

"Very funny. I think the tree will understand." Sending him a quick smirk, she broke open her cookie. "Aw," she said, frowning, "it's the same one. That's no fun."

"The restaurant must be at the bottom of the box or something. Either that or we're looking for the same thing."

"Well, in a way we are, aren't we?" Gill offered.

"Really?"

She met his eyes across the table. How on earth could one set of eyes have so many different hues? she asked herself, her breath catching. In the restaurant lighting, the gold and green combined to create a new shade of amber. She swore they flickered, too, like a candle.

"Isn't it obvious? We both want a successful party."

"Right. The party."

"Of course. If it's a hit, we both get what we want."

"I hope you're right."

Sitting back in his seat, he'd lowered his gaze. No longer able to see their color, Gill got a strange feeling the dancing amber in his eyes had disappeared. She didn't know why, but the idea bothered her.

Shaking off the notion, she raised her half-finished teacup. "Why don't we seal our good fortune with a toast? To a successful event."

"And—" he tapped his cup to hers "—to getting what we're looking for."

CHAPTER SEVEN

It was snowing when they left the restaurant. The flakes sparkled in the streetlights, like tiny white lights falling from the sky, and landed on Gill's hair and face. Oliver studied their sparkle. Moisture kissed her cheeks and eyelids, and when she smiled the drops shone from the glow on her face.

"First snow of the season. Pretty, isn't it?" She was referring to the snow.

"Gorgeous," Oliver replied. He wasn't. Surely she knew how good snow looked on her? Those perfectly shaped lips glimmered with moisture. He had the overwhelming urge to trace their shape with his tongue, to see if they tasted as sweet and perfect as they looked.

Thoughts like that had plagued him all evening. Ever since they'd stood under that mistletoe. His body tensed as he thought of how close they'd stood—so close he'd imagined feeling the fibers of her sweater brushing his shirt when she breathed. And that sweet mouth, so close for the taking....

Shoving his hands into his jacket pockets, he searched for a benign topic. Anything to keep his less professional thoughts at bay. "Hope my meter didn't run out while we were eating."

"Do you think we were in the restaurant that long?"

"Hard to say. I can't remember when we walked in."

That was another thing—suggesting dinner. A smart man would have backed away under that mistletoe, called her a cab, and said goodnight. But, no, he'd not only offered her a ride home but suggested dinner as well. What was he thinking? So what if her stomach had growled?

Truth was, he hadn't been thinking at all. The truck had been dark and the interior had smelled like evergreen. It had been as if they were still standing beneath the mistletoe. The words were out before he could stop them.

He unlocked his truck, then held the door for her to hop in, which she did, sliding across the faded leather seat with ease. He hadn't expected her to look as at home as she did in a pickup truck. It surprised him to see how comfortable she looked, with her cashmere coat wrapped around her legs. Her long, slender jean-clad legs.

Quickly he shut the door. No matter. Soon as he slid into the driver's seat, sealing them both into the close dark space, the thoughts returned.

She, on the other hand, was thinking about business. About "getting what she wanted." He could think unseemly thoughts about licking off snowflakes all he liked; she was busy thinking of her next move up the corporate ladder. Guys like him, guys driven by other motivations, didn't register on the upwardly mobile radar of women like her. Or if they did they didn't last long. He'd learned that lesson from Julia.

"Where to?" he asked, starting the car.

"Beacon and River," she replied. "It's across from the Comm—"

"I know the address." The answer came out far more abruptly than he'd intended, causing her to tense in response.

"Is that a problem?" she asked.

"Why would there be a problem?" Just because with those three words life had managed to dump a virtual bucket of cold water on his thoughts. Just in case he didn't remember the lesson, apparently.

"I don't know. You sounded annoyed. If it's the traffic this time of night…"

"It's not the traffic." Nor was it her fault where she lived. *Or how.* "I had a friend who lived in that neighborhood, is all."

"Oh." She fell silent, but he could feel her eyes on him. "From the tone, I'm going to guess the friendship changed, not the address."

"You could say that."

They made their way through traffic in awkward silence. Oliver watched as the landscape gradually changed to the business district. That was Boston. Parking lots and neighborhood stores gave way to insurance company high-rises and, eventually, the luxury of Back Bay. The buildings became grander—refurbished rather than old, or sparkling new with historic overtones, since the Back Bay forbade modern-looking construction. Commuters picked their way toward train stations, many carrying shopping bags along with their briefcases.

In the next seat, Gill shifted her weight. She hadn't said a word since they'd discussed her address. His fault, he thought guiltily. His tone hadn't been exactly warm and encouraging.

"Lot of people out shopping," he noted. "Got your Christmas shopping done yet?"

As an attempt at conversation it was lame, but apparently good enough—because Gill jumped at the bait. "Not even close. Fortunately I only have to buy for Gwen and hers."

Oliver noticed her voice changed when she talked about her sister. It grew softer, more indulgent. She'd had a similar tone when talking about the Teaberry trees. He also noticed she didn't mention parents. "I'll probably do what I do every year. Wait till the last minute, then go overboard spoiling everyone. How about you?"

"I've got some stuff for the kids at the center—and Maria, of course."

"Of course." She was looking at him again. "No family? Or have you simply not gotten to them yet?"

"My father and I don't really—we don't celebrate together."

"Sorry."

"Don't be. We're both happier for it. He's free to drink the day away, and I'm free not to watch."

"Ouch."

"Sorry. I'm not sure why I said that." The words had been out before he'd realized what he was saying. He *never* talked about his father. Why he chose to now he had no idea.

"Hey, if it's the truth…"

"Oh, it's the truth all right. If not for the center… I grew up a block away from the place," he elaborated.

He felt as much as saw the understanding cresting on her features. "No wonder you're so dedicated to the place."

Dedicated wasn't a strong enough word. "The place saved my life. Showed me there was more than benders and unemployment in my future. In fact, it was a volunteer at the shelter who convinced me I had what it took to go to Harvard."

"You went to Harvard? As in Harvard University?" Disbelief laced the question, like it did whenever he mentioned his alma mater.

"No, Harvard Junior College," he shot back, the sarcasm a habit.

"Sorry."

"Don't be. You're not the first person to react that way. You going to ask the next question?"

"What next question?"

"What's a guy with an Ivy League education doing running a community center instead of a corporation?"

"The thought did cross my mind."

Of course it did. She was the one who'd left her hometown and never looked back. "I guess I wanted to make sure other kids got the same opportunities I did."

"Admirable." She sounded sincere enough that he believed she meant it. "Is Harvard where you met your friend? The one who lives near me?" She looked away when he tensed—a reaction he always had when Julia came up. "You can tell me to mind my own business if you prefer."

What the hell? He should, but, having already opened the door to his past, he might as well fully cross the threshold. "Julia was my fiancée."

"What happened?"

Oliver shrugged. "She wanted someone different. Someone I wasn't."

"Oh." The sympathetic silence that followed said everything else.

They arrived at Gill's block. Although not the fanciest building in the area, it was still upscale, and it had a great view of the Common. Amazingly, there was a parking spot across from her front door. Oliver grabbed it and shifted into "park."

Suddenly the cab of his truck felt dark and small again. Having bared his past, Oliver felt open and exposed, and Gill's presence was too close for comfort. "Here you go— home sweet home," he said, in a voice that sounded too boisterous.

"So it is," Gill replied. "Thanks for the ride. And for suggesting dinner."

"No problem."

She made no move to leave. Oliver wondered if she expected him to step out and open the door. That would be the gentlemanly thing to do. He was about to when she spoke again. "Frog Pond's crowded tonight."

Following her gaze, he saw the glow coming from the rink. "We're taking the kids there on Sunday," he replied. "Part of our plan to expose them to new experiences. Believe it or not, a lot of them have never been here—despite growing up in the city."

"Then it's good that you're exposing them to new experiences," she replied.

"I wish I could do it more often, but unfortunately—"

"The budget only goes so far?"

"I must sound like a broken record."

"A little, but I understand why." They locked eyes for a second, then she looked away.

Oliver could see her fiddling with the strap on her pocketbook.

After a couple a beats, she added, "This party will bring in a lot of donations."

"I hope you're right."

"I'll talk to Peter McNabb about including a more overt solicitation for donations in the press materials. I'll also recommend he make a sizeable one himself."

"Buy himself some goodwill?" Oliver teased.

"I was thinking more like buying a new van." She smiled, her teeth bright in the dark. "Best way to change his image is to put his money where his mouth is, right?"

"Right." He shifted his weight, wondering if he was the only one dragging this goodbye out, or if she felt the same sense of hesitancy. From the way she fiddled with her purse strap it seemed so. "You never said what it is *you* get out of all this," he said. "Back in the restaurant, we toasted us both getting what we were looking for, but you never said what it was. Don't tell me you're looking for a new van, too?"

In the closeness, her laugh sounded soft, like a sigh. "There's a vice presidency opening at the agency after the first of the new year. I'm one of two candidates up for the position. I do a good enough job, and the job could be mine."

Yup they were, just another rung on her ladder. "That's important to you, isn't it?"

"Absolutely." There was a note of defensiveness to her tone; he'd chipped a nerve. "This has been my plan for as long as I can remember."

"To be vice president of Rosenthal Public Relations?"

"To be a success."

"You're not now?"

"You can always be more." Her voice dropped a notch. "I didn't have a center growing up. I only had myself."

"And your sister."

There was another, even softer laugh. "Gwen is amazing, but she and my mother were more accepting of our circumstances than I was. *I hated them.*" The last three words were said more harshly than he'd ever heard her speak, even when hurling insults at him. "I won't settle. Not ever."

No, Oliver thought to himself, he didn't suppose she would. The realization saddened him. "I hope you get what you want, then."

She leaned forward and looked him square in the eye. "I always do."

"I'm not surprised."

Oliver couldn't help himself. She was so close, so tantalizingly close. The sweet evergreen scent still clung to her. Like Christmas. He slipped a hand into her hair, the strands like damp silk flowing through his fingers. She gasped, her perfect mouth making a perfect O.

It was a bad idea. A very, very bad idea. Because now his palm was caressing her cheek, his thumb tugging her bottom lip.

"I don't think…"

Her protest was breathy, weak, and not very convincing. But it was enough to break the spell. With painful reluctance he pulled away. He turned and gripped the steering wheel with both hands. "Goodnight, Gill."

"Goodnight." She offered him an apologetic smile and slipped out the door.

He waited until she'd climbed her front steps and disappeared through her front door before pulling away. For a crazy second he thought she looked back in his direction—even imagined it was in regret—but knew it merely wishful thinking. In her protest, Gill had voiced what they both knew. Business didn't mesh with pleasure. As she'd said so clearly, Gill McKenzie was all about business and success. He'd made the mistake of asking a woman to choose once before; he'd be a fool to put himself in a position to lose again.

"Some of the kids have limited family, some have no family at all. More than one have lost brothers or sisters to violence."

As Oliver talked, the TV reporter nodded sympathetically, her heavily lined eyes moist with emotion.

Off camera, in the entrance hall of the community room, Gill was fighting a few tears herself. Oliver was doing magnificently. Handsome and sincere in selling the center's mission. He'd even made sure Peter McNabb received credit for funding their work, painting the tarnished businessman as a friend to the community.

She smiled. He'd done that for her, she was sure.

Since that night in his truck she and Oliver had kept their relationship on the most professional of planes. No touching, no personal conversations. Which was good, because she had no business thinking otherwise. She didn't have time for dating. She wasn't interested in anything but getting that promotion.

She listened as Oliver continued, relaying how they'd created the center's basketball team in response to a drive-by shooting at one of the playgrounds. "It's all about giving kids a home base," he was saying.

His dedication was beyond admirable. He'd built something here. Something he could be truly proud of. A family, almost.

That nagging sensation from before returned. Odd, but she seemed to be feeling it more and more. Though still vague, it was definitely stronger, increasing that restless sensation. Almost as if she'd forgotten something. She'd run down her to-do list at least a dozen times, but nothing glaring popped out at her.

Maybe she was feeling anxious on Stephanie's behalf? Despite the fact the Remaillard launch was next week, her rival didn't seem fazed at all. In fact this morning Gill had overheard her making plans for a ski weekend. Goodness knew if *she* had had that project she wouldn't have taken a weekend off. Not that she took weekends off to begin with.

On the other side of the camera, Oliver and the reporter were wrapping up. "You've given our viewers a lot to think about," the reporter said.

"Hopefully that'll mean donations," Oliver replied.

"Oh, I have no doubt you'll get a few." She nodded toward her camera crew. "Let's get some shots of these trees. This enchanted forest idea is terrific."

"It did turn out pretty good, didn't it?"

He shot a look in Gill's direction. She smiled.

"How do you think the interview went?" he asked, once the reporter and her crew had turned their attention.

"I think Roberta's right; you're going to attract quite a few donations. Your commitment really shines through. The center's lucky to have you fighting its corner." Anyone would be, she caught herself thinking.

He smiled, those eyes of his warm and something more. "You, too. You weren't kidding when you said the center would benefit. I guess I…" he rubbed the back of his neck, a now familiar gesture "…owe you another apology."

"A thank-you will suffice."

"Thank you."

"You're welcome."

The air between them settled. Gill wasn't sure what to say next. She should move, head over to where Roberta was shooting, but she couldn't seem to move. Oliver's close presence had her pinned.

"Good thing Carlos isn't here," he added with a grin. His eyes looked upward.

Following, Gill saw the mistletoe above them. "Think he'd take advantage?"

"A fellow would be foolish if he didn't."

In a flash they were back in Oliver's truck, with the dark, evergreen-scented air swirling around them. Gill swore she could feel him move closer. "I suppose a fellow would." She ran a tongue over her lower lip.

"Oliver? Can we get a couple shots of you moving the kids' trees around?" Roberta called over. "I want to get some B roll footage."

Was that reluctance or relief crossing his face? Relief, she decided. On both their parts. Because business didn't mix with pleasure. It simply didn't.

And yet, as she watched Oliver cross the room, the restless vagueness returned.

"Did I see the *Eyewitness News* truck driving away?" Maria walked into the community room shaking snow from her jacket. "What happened? Something wrong?"

Oliver was in the middle of moving the mini-trees back to their original places. "Nothing's wrong," he replied. "Gill convinced them to do a piece on the party."

"Wow—second reporter in three days. She's good."

"That she is." Very good. Though right now his mind was more on her standing beneath the mistletoe. Since the other night in his truck he hadn't been able to shake her spell. Simple things, like the smell of pine or a piece of stray tinsel, and *boom!* He was thinking of her.

"Gill came with them?"

"She wanted to make sure the reporter got her facts straight."

"Oh."

"What, oh?"

"Nothing," Maria replied, in a voice that said anything but.

Oliver set down the tree he was carrying and looked her straight on, giving her what he hoped was a mirror image of her intimidating stare.

"I can't help noticing she's been here a lot this week. Every day, in fact."

Yes, she had. Which didn't help keep her out of his head. "The party's only a week away. She wants to make sure things are done right."

The volunteer arched her brow. "Why? Doesn't she trust us?"

"She does. She's just hands-on."

"Hands-on, huh? Is that what we're calling it now?"

Oliver shot her a scowl that had her tossing a fiercer one back.

"Don't give me that look. I've seen you two looking at each other. This party ain't the only thing Ms. McKenzie's interested in."

Trying his best to ignore the way his gut jumped at Maria's pronouncement, Oliver shook his head. "Nice try, Maria."

"You gonna tell me you don't like her?"

"Doesn't matter." One of Becky's decorations fell off its branch. He bent down to retrieve it. "I know her type. Come the day after the party, she'll move on to bigger and better things."

"Wow, you're harsh. She seems really dedicated to helping the center."

She's dedicated to getting a promotion, Oliver thought to himself. He *had* to think that way. He had to remind himself that all her hard work was for personal gain. Otherwise he'd fall more under Gill's spell, and he was already treading a very thin line.

"Not harsh, Maria. Realistic."

His friend folded her coat over her arm, taking a long time to smooth the nylon material. "I think maybe you've been in the neighborhood too long. For a guy who preaches the sky's the limit to his kids, you're pretty jaded."

CHAPTER EIGHT

AFTER a week of off-and-on snow showers, Sunday found itself bright with sunshine. Gill found herself staring at the blue cloudless sky while sitting at her desk. Having spent so much time this week working on the McNabb party, she'd fallen behind with other projects. As a result, she had a small mountain of paperwork to get through—e-mails, client correspondence, and one new client proposal—but she couldn't concentrate. Restlessness had taken hold. All of a sudden her apartment felt too empty. She thought about calling Gwen, but her sister would be busy selling Christmas trees with Drew and their family.

Family. The word unsettled her more, made the apartment feel that much more lacking. She needed to do something, occupy herself somehow, but work didn't appeal to her.

Her gaze drifted across the street, to the public Commons and the crowds making their way to the Frog Pond. Oliver had said he was taking the kids skating today. She wondered if he was there yet.

Why? It's not like you're joining them.

She opened an e-mail from Elliot Rosenthal. He wanted a report on year-end activities. Great, another project.

Her eyes went back to the window. She bet Oliver was a good skater. He looked like an athlete. She could picture him now, leading kids by the hand around the pond. It'd be fun to watch.

What the heck? A short break wouldn't hurt. Might even quell the restlessness.

It wasn't until she reached the rink entrance and her pulse sped up that she admitted her true motive: a chance to see Oliver. Why she'd pretended otherwise was beyond her; she'd been making up excuses to see him all week long. Although during the week she cloaked her motives behind business excuses. What would she say today? Maybe she should go back before Oliver got the wrong idea.

She was just about to turn around when she heard, "Look, it's the tree lady!" Carlos, the mistletoe plotter, stumbled toward her. He wore a protective helmet and gripped the guardrail with both hands. His grin was brighter than the sun. "You ice skating, too?"

"Carlos, her name is Miss McKenzie, not the tree lady," Oliver skated up behind him, wearing a thick coat and a battered ice hockey helmet that covered his sandy brown hair. He managed to look simultaneously dashing and silly.

"Nice helmet," Gill remarked.

"Isn't it, though? It's what all the cool skaters are wearing—right, Carlos?" He knocked playfully on top of the boy's helmet. "Safety first. We don't want anyone cracking their head on the ice."

Watching the exchange, Gill felt her heart flip-flop. His obvious affection for the kids was something she was quickly coming to adore about him.

She realized he'd turned his smile on her. Catching his gaze, she smiled back. The winter air disappeared in a wash of warmth. "I was working and remembered you were taking the kids skating, so I thought I'd take a break and see how things were going."

"The kids are having a blast."

"I can skate backwards," Carlo piped in. "Watch." Still holding on to the railing, the boy took several baby steps to the rear. He looked so ridiculously proud of himself Gill had to laugh.

"Nice job, pal."

"You going to skate, too? You can be my partner."

"That's a nice offer, Carlos, but I—uh..."

"Ms. McKenzie already promised to be *my* partner."

Gill looked to Oliver, whose eyes had taken on an expectant light. He smiled and reached out a hand. "What do you say, angel? If you're worried about falling, I'll catch you."

Too late, Gill thought, her insides tumbling.

Ten minutes later she found herself sitting on a bench while Oliver laced her rented skates. "Do I get a helmet, too?" she teased.

"Do you need one?"

"No, but I wouldn't want to give the kids the wrong impression."

"Don't worry about them. I'm sure they'd prefer you kept the snow bunny look." He grinned and smoothed his palms around her ankle. "I know I do."

Gill's insides tumbled a little more. She reached for the hand he offered. "It's been a while since I've been on skates," she warned him. "I'm going to be a little rusty. You better keep your promise to catch me."

"Believe me, I will. I never break a promise."

No, she thought, from what she'd seen these past couple of weeks, he didn't. The knowledge made her feel safe and protected. Oliver was definitely a man you could count on. A good man. The kind of person a woman would be lucky to have in her life.

Except you're not looking for a relationship, remember? You've got bigger fish to fry.

"You don't look so rusty to me."

Lost in thought as she'd been, she hadn't realized they were already navigating the ice. Oliver still held her hand. His gloved fingers wrapped around hers felt so natural.

"I think I've been misled. You skate better than me."

Doubtful. Just as she'd expected, he moved on the ice with the natural grace of an athlete. "What can I say? I played a mean game of pond hockey in my day."

"Pond hockey, huh? Somehow I pictured you more the figure skating type."

"Nah, I left that to my stepsisters."

"I thought it was only you and your twin?"

They must have hit a chip in the surface, because she stumbled slightly. Oliver's strong hand steadied her from behind. The comment came out unconsciously. "That's because as far as my father is concerned my sister and I don't exist."

"Sorry."

"Don't be," she said, cutting off his sympathetic expression before it could take hold. "That chapter in my life closed when I left Towering Pines. I'm a different person now." The pronouncement didn't feel as certain as usual. Probably because she was reliving a childhood activity.

"Well," Oliver said, giving her ponytail a playful tug, "he certainly couldn't ignore you today. That ski jacket is the pinkest creation I've ever seen. Is that standard color for pond hockey?"

"Oh, look who's talking, Mr. Fashion Statement." She gave him a nudge with her shoulder.

He pretended to stumble a little, pulling her close. Their bodies slipped together in perfect alignment. "That how they check in pond hockey?" he asked. His breath was warm and moist against her cheek.

She turned, bringing her lips inches from his. "You'd be surprised how tough those games got."

"I like surprises," he replied.

"Miss McKenzie, watch!" Becky came stumbling by, more walking than skating behind a plastic milk crate.

"Looking good!" Gill called out. "Try taking a break between steps and see what happens. Step, step, step, glide."

The little girl followed the directions and glided half a foot before catching her balance. "Hey! I skated! Carlos, look! I can skate."

Suddenly Gill found herself surrounded by kids from the center, all clamoring for instructions. For the next thirty minutes she held an impromptu and not very accurate skating lesson. By the end the kids weren't much better than when they'd started, but they could all chant, "Step, step, step, glide!" and everyone laughed. A lot.

Gill decided she'd laughed the most. If someone had told her last week she'd be having the time of her life ice skating with a bunch of kids, she'd have told them they were crazy. She would have told them she was too busy to waste an afternoon like that. But today...today the decision felt natural. Like holding Oliver's hand.

Speaking of which, while he'd relinquished physical contact, Oliver's presence had stayed with her the entire afternoon. She'd needed only to look up to catch his smile or see his warm expression, and she could feel him.

"You look like you could use a hot cocoa," a familiar voice purred in her ear.

She wished she could relish the warm body behind her, that they were alone so she could lean up against him. "Sounds good to me."

Leaving the kids to practice, they made their way side by side to the concession stand. Gill could feel the back of Oliver's hand brush hers, and she wondered what he'd say if she entwined her fingers with his here, off the ice. She settled for giving his hair a tussle when he removed his helmet. "You better put a hat on that damp hair or you'll catch a chill."

He leaned into her space, coming dangerously close. "Then I'll have to find a way to warm up."

Shivers that had nothing to do with the cold danced down Gill's spine. Lack of personal space wasn't the only danger they were flirting with. Looking into Oliver's eyes, she saw a heat that told her their thoughts were the same.

"Fresh air agrees with you," he said, his eyes dipping to her mouth.

"You, too."

For a moment it looked as if he would lean closer. Instead, he quickly pulled back. "Heads up, we've been spotted."

"Mr. Oliver, can *we* get cocoa?" Carlos burst upon them, nearly falling as he hit the lip of the rink. "I'm thirsty."

Several other kids echoed the request.

"I have to pee, too," Becky added.

After much discussion, begging and disorder, it was decided Gill and another two chaperons would take restroom duty while Oliver and Maria would order the group hot chocolate.

Standing in the crowd at the refreshment stand, Oliver pretended not to notice Maria giving him the eye.

"Someone's having a good time," she said, clearly not deterred.

"Isn't that the point of a field trip?" he replied.

"I'm not talking about the kids. Interesting Gill showed up, don't you think?"

"Not really. She lives across the street. The kids asked her to stay." He didn't want to think about how excited he'd been to see her standing there. Like a teenage kid. She had to be the most beautiful woman at the rink. Even if she hadn't been wearing Day-Glo pink he wouldn't be able to tear his eyes off her. Every smile she shot in his direction went straight to his gut. It was ridiculous, but his insides swelled with pride that this gorgeous creature was looking at *him*.

"We should get chips to go with the drinks," he said to Maria. "The kids have to be hungry."

"Stop dodging the conversation. Why don't you just admit you like her?"

Admitting it wasn't the problem. He *knew* he liked her. Hell, watching her with the kids today, he'd begun to more than like her. "Okay, I like her. You satisfied?"

"From the looks of things she likes you, too."

Yeah, she did. That was the real problem. Every time he looked in her face and saw a desire matching his, the free-fall feeling he got terrified him. Say they gave in to their feelings—what then? A woman like Gill belonged in a world with designer clothes and luxury apartments. How long before she tired of a man whose life was anything but? How long before she dumped him for bigger and better?

Out of the corner of his eye, he saw a flash of pink approaching. "How about we just focus on the kids and leave my personal life for another day?"

"Okay." His friend sighed. "But I think you're missing the boat."

Better to miss then have to disembark, Oliver replied in his head.

There was only one picnic table available, so they did their best to crowd in. Playing the gentleman, Oliver stood to the side, intending to let everyone else rest, but Gill scooted over, making space.

"Here," she said patting the bench, "there's still space. If you don't mind squishing up against me."

With the entire table looking, he had no choice. He perched on the corner. Even then Gill's body nestled next to his cozily. The contact sent his nerve-endings into overdrive. From the look flashing in her eyes, it did hers, too.

God help him, but resisting was getting near impossible.

The group drank their cocoa and enjoyed the warmth. With Christmas around the corner, most of the conversation focused on the upcoming holiday. The younger kids, like Becky, still believed in Santa and looked forward to finding presents under the tree Christmas morning. Fortunately, the older kids were polite enough to keep the secret. One of them asked Gill what she was doing for Christmas.

"Are you going to visit the magic trees?" Becky asked.

"Actually, I am. My sister lives on the farm where they grow."

The word farm started a slew of questions, about chickens and milking cows and other stuff. Oliver watched as Gill answered all of them. She shared what it was like to take a sleigh ride, and cut down your own Christmas tree. By the time she got to Christmas morning and how she and her sister baked apple muffins, Oliver was as enchanted as the kids.

"Sounds like a great time," he said.

"It is," she replied. "Though thanks to work, I probably won't get to stay more than a day, maybe two, before coming back."

"But you're coming to our party, right?" Carlos asked.

"Are you kidding? Wild horses couldn't keep me away. It's going to be the highlight of my holidays. Well, that—" she tugged Becky's ponytail "—and Santa."

"So you'll definitely be there?" the boy prodded.

"I promise," Gill replied.

"Cool." There was a gleam in his charge's eye Oliver recognized all too well. The boy was smitten.

Get in line, Carlos, he thought, stealing a glance at the woman next to him. *Get in line.*

CHAPTER NINE

FOR as long as Gill could remember, one day had been the same as another. But, come Sunday night, she found herself finally understanding the phrase "weekend regret."

The day had flown by. Not in a blurry haze, like when she was engrossed in work, but in a "the hours are too short" kind of way she remembered from childhood. In fact, today she felt like a kid again. Energized and carefree in a way she hadn't felt in a long time.

Skating had brought back memories, too. She couldn't believe the stories she'd shared with the kids. Yet reliving her small-town roots hadn't disturbed her the way it normally did. Maybe because the kids had seemed genuinely interested. They'd listened to her stories as if they meant something. As if *she* meant something.

Huh, imagine that.

And then there was Oliver. Flirty, sexy, amazing Oliver, whose encouraging smile made her feel like the belle of the ball. Who knew one person's expression could make a person feel so special? Closing her eyes, she conjured up his face, enjoying the thrill the image sent through her.

Maybe Gwen's romantic streak had a point after all.

That thought was still rattling around her head when she walked into the office Monday. She was ticking off her day's to-do list, trying to figure out what excuse she could use to stop by the center and see Oliver. She was so engrossed, she failed to notice the chaos whirling around her. That was until Elliot Rosenthal's bellow ripped through the office.

"I'm going to kill her! Who on earth goes skiing four days before a major product launch? Gillian, get in here!"

The center was completely lit up when she stepped from the cab. Community league basketball. Oliver had mentioned something last night. Gill winced. She'd purposely waited until after pick-up time, so she and Oliver would be able to talk in private.

Oh, well, she thought with a sigh. It was the kids she was avoiding anyway. Adults she could handle.

She let herself in, noticing the kids had hung more snow-flakes in the entranceway. Her enchanted forest was growing by leaps and bounds. Peter McNabb would have a terrific backdrop for his photographs. She looked forward to reviewing the coverage.

Oliver was in his office, going over paperwork. He must have had a meeting, because instead of his usual sweater and corduroys he wore a black suit and tie, looking every inch the businessman he'd chosen not to be.

She took some hope in seeing him look that way. Maybe she was blowing this out of proportion? After all, Oliver was a professional; he understood the demands of a career. He'd understand her dilemma.

"This a bad time?" she asked.

His face brightened from the inside out the second he saw her. "Never a bad time for you. In fact, I was just thinking about ordering takeout. Feel like a little Chinese? We can test our fortunes again."

Gill could think of nothing she'd rather do than stay—especially with the way Oliver was smiling at her. Her stomach somersaulted at the knowledge she was about to let him down.

"I'm afraid I can't stay. I have to get back to work."

"Oh?" he replied with a frown. "What's up that you had to come by personally? There a problem?"

"A small one. Stephanie DeWitt had a skiing accident. She hit a tree and shattered her pelvis."

"That's terrible. Who's Stephanie DeWitt?"

"A co-worker. Actually…" She toed the floor with her boot. "She's the other woman under consideration for the vice presidency. With her out, I have to handle her project. It's a major aftershave launch for Remaillard Cosmetics. This means I'm pretty much a shoo-in for the promotion."

"That's great. That's what you wanted, right? Congratulations."

"Thanks."

"But you didn't come here just to share good news, did you?" His smile faded and his expression turned wary. The change made Gill uneasy. In that moment she knew her news wouldn't be taken well.

Might as well deliver the blow quickly. "The product launch is Thursday night."

"The same day as the McNabb Christmas party." Wariness gave way to something darker, reminding her of the anger she'd seen the day they met. "You promised the kids you'd be there."

And now she had to break that promise. Something, as he'd pointed out yesterday, he didn't believe in doing. But surely he had to see there were extenuating circumstances?

"Remaillard Cosmetics is our biggest account; a successful launch means a lot of new business."

He turned back to the paperwork on his desk. "What am I supposed to tell the kids? They think you're coming."

"Can't you tell them something came up?"

"You mean like a better offer?"

Gill didn't like where this conversation was headed. Or the coldness in his voice. Surely he had to understand that in the business scheme of things the Remaillard account had to come first? "I didn't choose for the launch to be held the same day as the party."

"No, you're simply choosing the launch over us."

"I have to. It's my job." Why was he making this sound so personal?

Because to him it was. *My kids. My center.* How many times did he use those phrases?

"Oliver, I didn't do this on purpose." She touched his shoulder. "I'll make it up to them."

"Sure you will. Unless another project comes up." Disbelief laced his every word. What hurt most was that he had wouldn't look at her. He simply shuffled the papers on his desk, his spine and his voice stiff and hard. "Look, I have a lot of paperwork to finish up. Do you need me to call you a cab?"

A cab? He was dismissing her? "Oliver—"

"What do you want me to say, Gill?" Finally he turned to face her. The look on his face made her wish he hadn't. "That I understand. Fine. I understand."

No, he didn't. Otherwise he'd see she truly didn't *have* a choice. She had to take this project. "Elliot Rosenthal is counting on me. I've worked too long and too hard to get where I am to mess up now."

"Of course you have."

He sounded so crisp and cold.

"This doesn't mean I don't…" She paused, unsure how to put her thoughts into words.

Before she could continue, Oliver held up his hand. "Don't, Gill. I'll tell the kids you had an emergency and couldn't work on the party anymore. Don't worry, they'll take it fine. They're used to disappointment."

Oliver listened to the angry click of Gill's boots fade in the distance. There was the slam of a car door, and he saw a pair of taillights disappear down the street. She'd asked the cab to wait. For some reason that only made him feel more annoyed. Feel more like a temporary stop.

"One more rung on the ladder of success," he mocked. He should have listened to his gut the day Gill walked in here, all high-heeled and high-powered.

Of course it was the kids he felt bad for. He'd always known she wouldn't stick around. That he and his center wouldn't be enough.

Paperwork had lost what little appeal it held. He needed to go home, crack a beer, and lose himself in a Celtics game. Tomorrow he'd figure out what to tell the kids.

He did his nightly tour, making sure the windows and doors were all locked and bolted. On the way back through the community room he stopped. Over the past two weeks the dingy space had been transformed. Garlands draped the windows. Ribbons and snowflakes hung from the ceiling. Surrounded by mini-trees, the Teaberry tree bathed the rest of the enchanted forest in soft light.

Slowly, he walked over and touched one of its branches. The pine fragrance reminded him of Gill. Longing welled up inside him. Longing stronger than he'd felt in a long time.

It was for the kids, he told himself. He was sad for the kids.

"Magical tree, my ass," he muttered, plucking a handful of needles. "If you're so magical, then make things right."

He let the needles fall on the floor.

The next two days passed in a blur of meetings and last-minute preparations. What Stephanie possessed in confidence and outward bravado, she apparently lacked in organization and follow-up skills. It took Gill half a day alone to figure out who was in charge of what task.

By the time she made it home to her apartment she was beyond exhausted. She crashed on her sofa. Even microwave popcorn was too much trouble tonight.

What she wouldn't give for some Kung Pao Chicken.

No, she wouldn't go there. According to Jeff, her stand-in on the center project, Oliver hadn't so much as mentioned her name during their meetings. He was obviously still upset. Knowing the chip on his shoulder, he'd probably stay that way forever. Just as well. Relationships and career didn't mix. If you could call what they'd had a relationship. What kind of relationship could you form in two weeks?

Gwen and Drew fell in love in four.

She wasn't Gwen. She wasn't in love. The hole in her chest was not a broken heart.

Her cell buzzed. Gill groaned. Not another text message. Couldn't she get five minutes to breathe?

She looked at the screen.

Thought you'd get a kick out of this video. Call when you're not so busy. Love, G.

The video was named "Claire Bear Snowman."

Gill loaded it up, and instantly her mood brightened. Her niece Claire was making a snowman—or, to be more accurate,

Drew was making the snowman. Claire was helping by throwing handfuls of snow at him.

"Come on, help Daddy push the snowball," she heard Drew say. He bent over to push, only to have Claire dump a handful of snow on the back of his neck. She could hear Gwen laughing behind the camera as Drew pretended to growl like a bear and chase Claire down. "This," he said, giving his stepdaughter a gigantic bear hug, "this is what it's all about."

Gill clicked off the video. Without the sound of taped laughter her apartment became very quiet and cold. She curled onto her side and stared at her mini-tree, unlit and browning from lack of water.

"I am a success," she said. The mini-tree and the apartment didn't answer.

CHAPTER TEN

THE ballroom of the Fairlane Hotel looked like a Parisian bistro. Gill had taken Stephanie's original idea, run with it, and with some last-minute tweaks turned it into a product launch for the books. The guests—members of the New York and Boston fashion elite—raved left and right. As did the executives from Remaillard.

"Magnificent!" one exclaimed, kissing her on each cheek Parisian-style.

Elliot Rosenthal was suitably blown away as well. "Nice recovery," he said, handing her a glass of champagne. "The kind of results you expect from a top executive."

There it was. He might as well have called her Madam Vice President. Tomorrow she expected he would call her into his office and bestow the title on her officially. Gill saluted his raised glass. She'd done it. She'd reached the next plateau.

The moment wasn't as celebratory as she'd hoped.

Smiling and nodding at the crowd, she walked the perimeter of the room, pausing to adjust a poster that had slipped on its display. *"His Present, Your Treat,"* the ad read. *"Make Every Night Christmas Eve."* Gill had bought a bottle for Drew. Someone might as well have fun.

"He's made me take him to see Santa Claus three times. I swear the boy has the longest Christmas list in America."

"Did you tell him Santa can't fit everything in his sleigh?"

"When I did, he said, 'That's okay, Mommy. I asked for a trailer, too.'"

Behind the poster, two women laughed at the story. Gill tried not to listen in, but the minute she heard the word *Santa* she found herself tuned in. A quick look at her watch told her "Santa" would have just arrived at the center. Peter McNabb probably had his hands full right about now.

Stop, Gillian. You weren't going to think about Oliver or the center tonight.

She continued on her route. Another poster on the other side of the room needed fixing. This time she overheard two couples.

"I try to be a disciplinarian, but one look at those big brown eyes and I melt. I can't help it."

"The way they look when you walk through the door at night. Makes coming home worthwhile."

Coming home worthwhile. The conversation continued—something about puppy school—but Gill was no longer listening. She was replaying Gwen's video in her memory. Drew had said something similar. Her brother-in-law ran a successful worldwide corporation; he was worth millions. Yet she never saw him happier than when he was doting on Gwen and Claire. When was the last time she'd been truly happy, outside of visiting her sister?

Ice skating with the kids. She smiled. Sharing Chinese food. Every time Oliver smiled at her.

Makes coming home worthwhile.

What did she have to come home to? Work and a dying miniature Christmas tree.

All these years trying not to be poor Gillian McKenzie, and her life sounded more pathetic than ever.

A hand tapped her shoulder. "Stéphane Remaillard is about to make his remarks," Ken the intern told her. "Elliot wanted you up on the dais with them."

"Sure. Be right there." Time for her moment of glory.

Worth coming home to.

You always succeed when you put your mind to it.

Gwen was right. Since when did she just let events sweep her along as if she didn't have a choice? If life didn't give you something, you went out and made your own magic.

Maybe it was time she followed her own advice and made herself happy.

Christmas music blasted from the DJ's speakers. The community center had never been fuller or more lively. Kids, both the center's and children of invited guests, ran amok, playing and laughing. Older kids danced. Peter McNabb, in Santa garb, glad-handed and posed for photos in front of the enchanted forest. Adults mingled and read literature on the center's work. More than one had seen the feature on television and had promised a check upon an introduction.

"Mr. Oliver!" Jamarcus ran up, brandishing a candy cane and a stuffed teddy bear. There was chocolate rimming his mouth. "Look what Santa gave me."

Oliver put aside his blues. "Good for you, Jamarcus."

"I also got chocolate from Maria."

"So I see." He barely got the response out before the toddler was off, searching for the next activity.

He had to hand it to her, Gill had pulled together a triumph for McNabb and the center.

Too bad she wasn't here to see her success. Then again, she was basking in another success tonight.

At least a dozen times he'd picked up the phone to call her, only to change his mind at the last minute. The problem was bigger than just her career aspirations. Hell, he understood workaholism better than anyone.

No, it was a matter of priorities. If she chose her career over her promise to the kids this time, who's to say she wouldn't make a similar choice again? Who's to say the next time he wouldn't be the thing that came up short?

Face it, Harrington, you cut bait because you were afraid she won't think you're good enough for her. Why not? Didn't Julia come to that same conclusion right before she walked out? Right after he refused to give up working at the center?

Only Gill wasn't Julia. She was far, far better.

And Gill didn't ask him to choose anything. He made the choice for her. Without giving her a chance.

For a guy who preaches the sky's the limit, you're pretty jaded. Maria's words came floating back to him. It was true. What kind of example was he for the kids if he was too afraid to take a chance himself?

Or rather, give Gill a chance?

A hand tugged the back of his suit jacket. He turned to see Becky and two other girls. "Carlos keeps dragging us under the mistletoe," they complained. "Can we slap him?"

"No," Oliver replied. He had to fight his chuckle. Carlos had been carrying out his mistletoe mission all night, much to the chagrin of Becky and the other girls. Although they didn't seem all that upset at the moment, despite their complaints. "I'll go talk to him and tell him to knock it off. Where is he?"

A look passed between the girls. "Hanging out in the doorway," one of them finally answered.

The better to catch unsuspecting girls; the kid wasn't stupid. "Don't worry," he told them. "I'll take care of everything."

"We know you will," Becky said, before the trio ran off giggling. Girls. They were a mystical lot.

He wove his way through the crowd to the doorway. The mistletoe had been the one part of the room he'd avoided until now. Looking at it only reminded him of Gill. A fresh bout of chagrin attacked him. As soon as he'd talked to Carlos he was definitely finding a phone. He'd leave a million messages if he had to.

Or maybe not. Halfway across the room, he froze.

There, under the mistletoe, stood Gill.

He recognized her red dress as a designer number from Newberry Street. Simple, but elegant, it needed no adornment other than her long blond hair. His heart began to race.

She'd changed her choice.

Gill's heart pounded in her chest. It had been ages since she'd sent the girls to get Oliver. What if he didn't believe their ruse? What if he saw her and didn't want to talk with her? Or, worse, what if she'd misread the emotions she'd seen in his eyes?

Suddenly she saw him. Standing stock-still in the crowd. Their eyes locked. Slowly, he began moving forward. Blood pounding in her ears, Gill counted his steps. Five. Six.

At last he reached her. "You came."

Gill nodded. "I made a promise. I had to keep it."

"The kids will be happy."

"Just the kids?"

With a shake of his head, Oliver moved a little closer. "Not just the kids. Me. I owe you an apology."

"You do?"

"For losing my temper. For misjudging you. I always saw this center as a sort of symbol of what I overcame. Except I'm beginning to realize I didn't escape my roots as much as I thought. When you chose your project over the party I felt... I took it personally. I felt like you thought the center wasn't good enough for you."

Rubbing the back of his neck, he dipped his head and toed the doorway threshold with that sheepish expression she adored. "That I wasn't good for you."

Not good enough? A lump rose in Gill's throat. Her handsome, confident Oliver didn't think he was good enough for *her?* He couldn't be more wrong.

"I compared you to Julia and that was wrong. I should have given you a chance. Do you think you can forgive me?"

He looked up, and the emotion she saw brimming in his eyes brought a lump to her throat. The tightness that had been gripping her lungs slowly melted through her, filling her with an emotion too light, too wonderful to describe. Forgive him? For what? Letting his past color his actions? Hadn't she been doing the very same thing?

"I can forgive you," she said with a smile, "if you can give me another chance."

"Oh, angel, I'll give you all the chances in the world." He paused, his happy expression suddenly growing confused. "What about the big product launch? Aren't you supposed to be there?"

"Uh-huh."

"Then why aren't—?"

Gill pressed her fingers to his lips. He was getting that inner glow she loved, and she was dying to touch him. "Being with you, being with the kids—it made me realize there's a little more to life than working twenty-four-seven. There's something to be said for having more in your life. *I* want more in my life."

"Same here," he replied.

Seeing the expectancy in his eyes, she knew without doubt what she needed to say next. He'd taken a chance and bared his soul. It was time for her to do the same. "I want *you* in my life."

Oliver moved closer. Gill took a deep breath. His eyes shone with emotion as they searched her face. Finally, after what seemed a thousand years, he answered. "Same here." Reaching out, he brushed her lower lip with his thumb. The caress reached to her heart. "I think I might be falling in love with you, angel."

Gill let out her breath. She hadn't misread those emotions after all. "Same here," she whispered.

"You know something else?" Oliver whispered back.

"What?" Gill was on cloud nine. No promotion, no words, nothing could possibly be more wonderful than what she'd just heard. Oliver Harrington was falling for her.

He slipped his arms around her waist and pulled her close. "You're under the mistletoe," he murmured against her lips.

"So I am," Gill responded with a smile. "What should we do about it?"

"I don't know about you, but I'm going to claim my woman before Carlos gets here."

Slanting his mouth over hers, he did just that.

EPILOGUE

One Year Later...

OUTSIDE the snowflakes had begun to fall. It looked as if Towering Pines would get a white Christmas after all. Curled into a corner of the sofa, Gill sipped her ginger tea with a smile. Across from her, this year's Teaberry tree glistened magically.

The sound of slippered footsteps drew her attention. "Took five readings of *Santa Mouse,* but Claire finally fell asleep," Gwen announced. "She wanted to know if Santa would leave the baby in her stocking."

She eased herself onto the sofa, sighing happily. Eight months pregnant, she glowed with maternal expectancy. "I swear she's as eager for the baby to arrive as Drew and I are. Of course part of me thinks she's confusing getting a baby sister with getting a pony."

"Knowing Drew, she'll get both."

"As well as a puppy, a kitten, and half the West Virgina Zoo. I swear that girl has him wrapped around her little finger."

"That a bad thing?" Gill asked.

"No," her twin replied, her eyes filling with love. "He's such a wonderful father. I can't wait to see him hold this baby."

It was true. Since meeting Gwen, Drew had turned into the consummate family man. *Just goes to show what love will do to a person,* Gill thought to herself, absently pressing a palm to her belly. She had her own Christmas secret she was planning to share tonight.

"Where *are* the boys anyway?" Gwen asked. "Still delivering trees?"

"Apparently so."

With Gwen so far along in her pregnancy, Drew had insisted she cut back on her work at the farm this season, so Oliver and Gill had flown down early to help out. True to his nature, Oliver had convinced Drew to have the leftover trees donated to local needy families.

"Shouldn't we spread some of the Teaberry magic around?" he'd teased.

She must have smiled—she'd been doing that a lot lately—because Gwen asked, "Penny for your thoughts?"

"I was thinking about the Teaberry legend. How we used to think the trees were magical."

"Well, they certainly brought *us* magic, didn't they?"

Gill shook her head. Even after four years of marriage, Gwen was still a hopeless, whimsical romantic. Before she could correct her, however, the front door opened and a trio of handsome, snow-covered men tromped in. All three were handsome as sin, but only one made her pulse quicken. She palmed her belly again while she watched Oliver untie his boots.

"Man, but I miss California," Brody said, shaking the snow from his baseball cap. Nearly twenty, he was the spitting image of his father. "You don't have to worry about getting your car stuck in snow out there."

"No, just traffic," Drew teased back.

"Very funny, Dad. I'm going to go call Susan; see if she's more sympathetic."

"You better hurry. Something might have happened since her last text message."

Brody stuck his tongue out before disappearing upstairs.

"I swear," Drew said, joining them in the living room, "those two are joined at the hip." He sat next to Gwen and gestured for her to raise her feet. "Did I miss storytime?" he asked, slipping off her slippers and massaging her feet.

"'Fraid so, but I won't be surprised if there's a round two."

"I'll take that one. You better get some sleep. She's going to be up at the crack of dawn."

"Urged on, no doubt, by her Christmas-loving daddy."

Gill was watching the exchange when she felt a pair of strong hands rest on her shoulders. "Miss me?" a voice whispered in her ear.

"Always," she whispered back.

Oliver nuzzled the crook of her neck, instantly sending tingles through her. They'd been married eight months now, and his touch still thrilled her as much as it had that first time. She suspected the sensation would never change.

"Did you get all your trees delivered?"

"Every one. Teaberry magic has now been distributed."

"Gill and I just were talking about the Teaberry legend," Gwen said. "She was going to tell me, like she does every year, that there's no such thing as magic trees. Right, sis?"

Looking around the room, Gill saw nothing but love and happiness flowing from the people in it. She looked at Drew and Gwen, expectant parents who'd found love and trust here at Teaberry Farms. Then there was the man standing behind her. Her husband. It was Christmas that had led her to his doorstep. Her life would be so empty had she not met him. She thought of the life they had created together, and how thrilled he would be when she told him he was going to become a father. Tonight, under a Teaberry Christmas tree.

"I don't know," she replied, her gaze traveling to the tree across the room. "Maybe there's some truth to that old legend after all."

* * * * *

HARLEQUIN Romance.

Coming Next Month

Available December 7, 2010

REQUEST YOUR FREE BOOKS!
2 FREE NOVELS PLUS 2
FREE GIFTS!

From the Heart, For the Heart

YES! Please send me 2 FREE Harlequin® Romance novels and my 2 FREE gifts (gifts are worth about $10). After receiving them, if I don't wish to receive any more books, I can return the shipping statement marked "cancel". If I don't cancel, I will receive 6 brand-new novels every month and be billed just $3.84 per book in the U.S. or $4.24 per book in Canada. That's a savings of 15% off the cover price! It's quite a bargain! Shipping and handling is just 50¢ per book.* I understand that accepting the 2 free books and gifts places me under no obligation to buy anything. I can always return a shipment and cancel at any time. Even if I never buy another book from Harlequin, the two free books and gifts are mine to keep forever.

116/316 HDN E7T2

Name	(PLEASE PRINT)
Address	Apt. #
City	State/Prov.	Zip/Postal Code

Signature (if under 18, a parent or guardian must sign)

Mail to the **Harlequin Reader Service:**
IN U.S.A.: P.O. Box 1867, Buffalo, NY 14240-1867
IN CANADA: P.O. Box 609, Fort Erie, Ontario L2A 5X3

Not valid for current subscribers to Harlequin Romance books.

**Are you a subscriber to Harlequin Romance books
and want to receive the larger-print edition?
Call 1-800-873-8635 or visit www.ReaderService.com.**

* Terms and prices subject to change without notice. Prices do not include applicable taxes. Sales tax applicable in N.Y. Canadian residents will be charged applicable provincial taxes and GST. Offer not valid in Quebec. This offer is limited to one order per household. All orders subject to approval. Credit or debit balances in a customer's account(s) may be offset by any other outstanding balance owed by or to the customer. Please allow 4 to 6 weeks for delivery. Offer available while quantities last.

Your Privacy: Harlequin Books is committed to protecting your privacy. Our Privacy Policy is available online at www.ReaderService.com or upon request from the Reader Service. From time to time we make our lists of customers available to reputable third parties who may have a product or service of interest to you. If you would prefer we not share your name and address, please check here. ☐

Help us get it right—We strive for accurate, respectful and relevant communications. To clarify or modify your communication preferences, visit us at www.ReaderService.com/consumerschoice.

HR10R2

HARLEQUIN®

A Romance

FOR EVERY MOOD™

Spotlight on

Classic

Quintessential, modern love stories
that are romance at its finest.

See the next page
to enjoy a sneak peek from
the Harlequin® Romance series.

*See below for a sneak peek from our classic
Harlequin® Romance® line.*

Introducing DADDY BY CHRISTMAS by Patricia Thayer.

MIA caught sight of Jarrett when he walked into the open
lobby. It was hard not to notice the man. In a charcoal
business suit with a crisp white shirt and striped tie covered
by a dark trench coat, he looked more Wall Street than
small-town Colorado.

Mia couldn't blame him for keeping his distance. He
was probably tired of taking care of her.

Besides, why would a man like Jarrett McKane be
interested in her? Why would he want to take on a woman
expecting a baby? Yet he'd done so many things for her.
He'd been there when she'd needed him most. How could
she not care about a man like that?

Heart pounding in her ears, she walked up behind him.
Jarrett turned to face her. "Did you get enough sleep last
night?"

"Yes, thanks to you," she said, wondering if he'd thought
about their kiss. Her gaze went to his mouth, then she
quickly glanced away. "And thank you for not bringing up
my meltdown."

Jarrett couldn't stop looking at Mia. Blue was definitely
her color, bringing out the richness of her eyes.

"What meltdown?" he said, trying hard to focus on what
she was saying. "You were just exhausted from lack of
sleep and worried about your baby."

He couldn't help remembering how, during the night,
he'd kept going in to watch her sleep. How strange was
that? "I hope you got enough rest."

She nodded. "Plenty. And you're a good neighbor for

coming to my rescue."

He tensed. Neighbor? *What neighbor kisses you like I did?* "That's me, just the full-service landlord," he said, trying to keep the sarcasm out of his voice. He started to leave, but she put her hand on his arm.

"Jarrett, what I meant was you went beyond helping me." Her eyes searched his face. "I've asked far too much of you."

"Did you hear me complain?"

She shook her head. "You should. I feel like I've taken advantage."

"Like I said, I haven't minded."

"And I'm grateful for everything…"

Grasping her hand on his arm, Jarrett leaned forward. The memory of last night's kiss had him aching for another. "I didn't do it for your gratitude, Mia."

Gorgeous tycoon Jarrett McKane has never believed in Christmas—but he can't help being drawn to soon-to-be-mom Mia Saunders! Christmases past were spent alone…and now Jarrett may just have a fairy-tale ending for all his Christmases future!

*Available December 2010,
only from Harlequin® Romance®.*

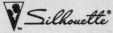

Sparked by Danger, Fueled by Passion.

RACHEL LEE
A Soldier's Redemption

When the Witness Protection Program fails at
keeping Cory Farland out of harm's way, ex-
marine Wade Kendrick steps in. As Cory's new
bodyguard, Wade has a plan for protecting her—
however falling in love was not part of his plan.

*Available in December
wherever books are sold.*

HARLEQUIN *Presents*

Bestselling Harlequin Presents® author

Julia James

brings you her most powerful book yet...

FORBIDDEN OR FOR BEDDING?

The shamed mistress...

Guy de Rochemont's name is a byword for wealth
and power—and now his duty is to wed.

Alexa Harcourt knows she can never be anything
more than *The de Rochemont Mistress.*

But Alexa—the one woman Guy wants—is also
the one woman whose reputation
forbids him to take her as his wife....

**Available from Harlequin Presents
December 2010**